Lord Macaulay

## Lays of ancient Rome

Ivry and the Armada

Lord Macaulay

**Lays of ancient Rome**
*Ivry and the Armada*

ISBN/EAN: 9783742800596

Manufactured in Europe, USA, Canada, Australia, Japa

Cover: Foto ©Andreas Hilbeck / pixelio.de

Manufactured and distributed by brebook publishing software
(www.brebook.com)

Lord Macaulay

**Lays of ancient Rome**

# LAYS OF ANCIENT ROME

WITH

## IVRY AND THE ARMADA

## BY LORD MACAULAY

*NEW EDITION*

LONDON
LONGMANS, GREEN, AND CO.
1874

# PREFACE.

THAT what is called the history of the Kings and early Consuls of Rome is to a great extent fabulous, few scholars have, since the time of Beaufort, ventured to deny. It is certain that, more than three hundred and sixty years after the date ordinarily assigned for the foundation of the city, the public records were, with scarcely an exception, destroyed by the Gauls. It is certain that the oldest annals of the commonwealth were compiled more than a century and a half after this destruction of the records. It is certain, therefore, that the great Latin writers of the Augustan age did not possess those materials, without which a trustworthy account of the infancy of the republic could not possibly be framed. Those writers own, indeed, that the chronicles to which they had access were filled with battles that were never fought, and Consuls that were never inaugurated; and we have abundant proof that, in these chronicles, events of the greatest importance, such as the issue of the war with Porsena, and the

issue of the war with Brennus, were grossly mis-
represented. Under these circumstances a wise
man will look with great suspicion on the legend
which has come down to us. He will perhaps be
inclined to regard the princes who are said to have
founded the civil and religious institutions of
Rome, the son of Mars, and the husband of Egeria,
as mere mythological personages, of the same class
with Perseus and Ixion. As he draws nearer and
nearer to the confines of authentic history, he will
become less and less hard of belief. He will admit
that the most important parts of the narrative have
some foundation in truth. But he will distrust
almost all the details, not only because they seldom
rest on any solid evidence, but also because he will
constantly detect in them, even when they are
within the limits of physical possibility, that peculiar character, more easily understood than defined,
which distinguishes the creations of the imagination from the realities of the world in which we
live.

The early history of Rome is indeed far more
poetical than anything else in Latin literature.
The loves of the Vestal and the God of War, the
cradle laid among the reeds of Tiber, the fig-tree,
the she-wolf, the shepherd's cabin, the recognition,
the fratricide, the rape of the Sabines, the death
of Tarpeia, the fall of Hostus Hostilius, the struggle
of Mettus Curtius through the marsh, the women

rushing with torn raiment and dishevelled hair
between their fathers and their husbands, the
nightly meetings of Numa and the Nymph by the
well in the sacred grove, the fight of the three
Romans and the three Albans, the purchase of the
Sibylline books, the crime of Tullia, the simulated
madness of Brutus, the ambiguous reply of the
Delphian oracle to the Tarquins, the wrongs of
Lucretia, the heroic actions of Horatius Cocles, of
Scævola, and of Clœlia, the battle of Regillus won
by the aid of Castor and Pollux, the defence of
Cremera, the touching story of Coriolanus, the still
more touching story of Virginia, the wild legend
about the draining of the Alban lake, the combat
between Valerius Corvus and the gigantic Gaul,
are among the many instances which will at once
suggest themselves to every reader.

In the narrative of Livy, who was a man of fine
imagination, these stories retain much of their
genuine character. Nor could even the tasteless
Dionysius distort and mutilate them into mere
prose. The poetry shines, in spite of him, through
the dreary pedantry of his eleven books. It is
discernible in the most tedious and in the most
superficial modern works on the early times of
Rome. It enlivens the dulness of the Universal
History, and gives a charm to the most meagre
abridgements of Goldsmith.

Even in the age of Plutarch,there were discern-

ing men who rejected the popular account of the
foundation of Rome, because that account appeared
to them to have the air, not of a history, but of a
romance or a drama.   Plutarch, who was dis-
pleased at their incredulity, had nothing better to
say in reply to their arguments than that chance
sometimes turns poet, and produces trains of
events not to be distinguished from the most
elaborate plots which are constructed by art.* But
though the existence of a poetical element in the
early history of the Great City was detected so
many years ago, the first critic who distinctly saw
from what source that poetical element had been
derived was James Perizonius, one of the most acute
and learned antiquaries of the seventeenth century.
His theory, which, in his own days, attracted little
or no notice, was revived in the present generation
by Niebuhr, a man who would have been the first
writer of his time, if his talent for communicating
truths had borne any proportion to his talent for
investigating them.   That theory has been adopted

* Ὑποπτον μὲν ἐνίοις ἐστὶ τὸ δραματικὸν καὶ πλασματῶδις· οὐ
δεῖ δὲ ἀπιστεῖν, τὴν τύχην ὁρῶντας, οἵων ποιημάτων δημιουργός
ἐστι.—*Plut. Rom.* viii.   This remarkable passage has been
more grossly misinterpreted than any other in the Greek
language, where the sense was so obvious.   The Latin version
of Cruserius, the French version of Amyot, the old English
version by several hands, and the later English version by
Langhorne, are all equally destitute of every trace of the
meaning of the original.   None of the translators saw even
that ποίημα is a poem.   They all render it an event.

by several eminent scholars of our own country, particularly by the Bishop of St. David's, by Professor Malden, and by the lamented Arnold. It appears to be now generally received by men conversant with classical antiquity; and indeed it rests on such strong proofs, both internal and external, that it will not be easily subverted. A popular exposition of this theory, and of the evidence by which it is supported, may not be without interest even for readers who are unacquainted with the ancient languages.

The Latin literature which has come down to us is of later date than the commencement of the Second Punic War, and consists almost exclusively of works fashioned on Greek models. The Latin metres, heroic, elegiac, lyric, and dramatic, are of Greek origin. The best Latin epic poetry is the feeble echo of the Iliad and Odyssey. The best Latin eclogues are imitations of Theocritus. The plan of the most finished didactic poem in the Latin tongue was taken from Hesiod. The Latin tragedies are bad copies of the masterpieces of Sophocles and Euripides. The Latin comedies are free translations from Demophilus, Menander, and Apollodorus. The Latin philosophy was borrowed, without alteration, from the Portico and the Academy; and the great Latin orators constantly proposed to themselves as patterns the speeches of Demosthenes and Lysias.

But there was an earlier Latin literature, a
literature truly Latin, which has wholly perished,
which had, indeed, almost wholly perished long
before those whom we are in the habit of regarding
as the greatest Latin writers were born. That
literature abounded with metrical romances, such
as are found in every country where there is much
curiosity and intelligence, but little reading and
writing. All human beings, not utterly savage,
long for some information about past times, and
are delighted by narratives which present pictures
to the eye of the mind. But it is only in very
enlightened communities that books are readily
accessible. Metrical composition, therefore, which,
in a highly civilised nation, is a mere luxury, is,
in nations imperfectly civilised, almost a necessary of life, and is valued less on account of the
pleasure which it gives to the ear, than on account
of the help which it gives to the memory. A man
who can invent or embellish an interesting story,
and put it into a form which others may easily
retain in their recollection, will always be highly
esteemed by a people eager for amusement and information, but destitute of libraries. Such is the
origin of ballad-poetry, a species of composition
which scarcely ever fails to spring up and flourish
in every society, at a certain point in the progress
towards refinement. Tacitus informs us that songs
were the only memorials of the past which the

ancient Germans possessed. We learn from Lucan and from Ammianus Marcellinus that the brave actions of the ancient Gauls were commemorated in the verses of Bards. During many ages, and through many revolutions, minstrelsy retained its influence over both the Teutonic and the Celtic race. The vengeance exacted by the spouse of Attila for the murder of Siegfried was celebrated in rhymes, of which Germany is still justly proud. The exploits of Athelstane were commemorated by the Anglo-Saxons, and those of Canute by the Danes, in rude poems, of which a few fragments have come down to us. The chants of the Welsh harpers preserved, through ages of darkness, a faint and doubtful memory of Arthur. In the Highlands of Scotland may still be gleaned some relics of the old songs about Cuthullin and Fingal. The long struggle of the Servians against the Ottoman power was recorded in lays full of martial spirit. We learn from Herrera that, when a Peruvian Inca died, men of skill were appointed to celebrate him in verses, which all the people learned by heart, and sang in public on days of festival. The feats of Kurroglou, the great free-booter of Turkistan, recounted in ballads composed by himself, are known in every village of Northern Persia. Captain Beechey heard the Bards of the Sandwich Islands recite the heroic achievements of Tamehameha, the most illustrious of their kings.

Mungo Park found in the heart of Africa a class of singing men, the only annalists of their rude tribes, and heard them tell the story of the victory which Damel, the negro prince of the Jaloffs, won over Abdulkader, the Mussulman tyrant of Foota Torra. This species of poetry attained a high degree of excellence among the Castilians, before they began to copy Tuscan patterns. It attained a still higher degree of excellence among the English and the Lowland Scotch, during the fourteenth, fifteenth, and sixteenth centuries. But it reached its full perfection in ancient Greece; for there can be no doubt that the great Homeric poems are generically ballads, though widely distinguished from all other ballads, and indeed from almost all other human compositions, by transcendent sublimity and beauty.

As it is agreeable to general experience that, at a certain stage in the progress of society, ballad-poetry should flourish, so is it also agreeable to general experience that, at a subsequent stage in the progress of society, ballad-poetry should be undervalued and neglected. Knowledge advances: manners change: great foreign models of composition are studied and imitated. The phraseology of the old minstrels becomes obsolete. Their versification, which, having received its laws only from the ear, abounds in irregularities, seems licentious and uncouth. Their simplicity appears beggarly

when compared with the quaint forms and gaudy
colouring of such artists as Cowley and Gongora.
The ancient lays, unjustly despised by the learned
and polite, linger for a time in the memory of the
vulgar, and are at length too often irretrievably
lost.   We cannot wonder that the ballads of Rome
should have altogether disappeared, when we
remember how very narrowly, in spite of the invention of printing, those of our own country and
those of Spain escaped the same fate.   There is
indeed little doubt that oblivion covers many
English songs equal to any that were published by
Bishop Percy, and many Spanish songs as good as
the best of those which have been so happily translated by Mr. Lockhart.   Eighty years ago England
possessed only one tattered copy of Childe Waters
and Sir Cauline, and Spain only one tattered copy
of the noble poem of the Cid.   The snuff of a
candle, or a mischievous dog, might in a moment
have deprived the world for ever of any of those fine
compositions. Sir Walter Scott, who united to the
fire of a great poet the minute curiosity and patient
diligence of a great antiquary, was but just in time
to save the precious relics of the Minstrelsy of the
Border.   In Germany, the lay of the Nibelungs had
been long utterly forgotten, when, in the eighteenth
century, it was, for the first time, printed from a
manuscript in the old library of a noble family.
In truth, the only people who, through their whole

passage from simplicity to the highest civilisation,
never for a moment ceased to love and admire their
old ballads, were the Greeks.

That the early Romans should have had ballad-
poetry, and that this poetry should have perished,
is therefore not strange. It would, on the contrary,
have been strange if these things had not come to
pass; and we should be justified in pronouncing
them highly probable, even if we had no direct
evidence on the subject. But we have direct evidence of unquestionable authority.

Ennius, who flourished in the time of the Second
Punic War, was regarded in the Augustan age as
the father of Latin poetry. He was, in truth, the
father of the second school of Latin poetry, the
only school of which the works have descended to
us. But from Ennius himself we learn that there
were poets who stood to him in the same relation
in which the author of the romance of Count
Alarcos stood to Garcilaso, or the author of the
'Lytell Geste of Robyn Hode' to Lord Surrey.
Ennius speaks of verses which the Fauns and the
Bards were wont to chant in the old time, when
none had yet studied the graces of speech, when
none had yet climbed the peaks sacred to the
Goddesses of Grecian song. 'Where,' Cicero
mournfully asks, 'are those old verses now?' *

* 'Quid? Nostri veteres versus ubi sunt?

. . . . . . . "Quos olim Fauni vatesque canebant.

Contemporary with Ennius was Quintus Fabius Pictor, the earliest of the Roman annalists. His account of the infancy and youth of Romulus and Remus has been preserved by Dionysius, and contains a very remarkable reference to the ancient Latin poetry. Fabius says that, in his time, his countrymen were still in the habit of singing ballads about the Twins. 'Even in the hut of Faustulus,'—so these old lays appear to have run,—'the children of Rhea and Mars were, in port and in spirit, not like unto swineherds or cowherds, but such that men might well guess them to be of the blood of Kings and Gods.' *

> Cum neque Musarum scopulos quisquam superârat,
> Nec dicti studiosus erat." '             *Brutus,* xviii.

The Muses, it should be observed, are Greek divinities. The Italian Goddesses of verse were the Camœnœ. At a later period, the appellations were used indiscriminately; but in the age of Ennius there was probably a distinction. In the epitaph of Nævius, who was the representative of the old Italian school of poetry, the Camœnæ, not the Muses, are represented as grieving for the loss of their votary. The 'Musarum scopuli' are evidently the peaks of Parnassus.

Scaliger, in a note on Varro (*De Lingua Latina,* lib. vi.), suggests, with great ingenuity, that the Fauns, who were represented by the superstition of later ages as a race of monsters, half gods and half brutes, may really have been a class of men who exercised in Latium, at a very remote period, the same functions which belonged to the Magians in Persia and to the Bards in Gaul.

* Οἱ δὲ ἀνδρωθέντες γίνονται, κατά τι ἀξίωσιν μορφῆς καὶ φρονήματος ὄγκον, οὐ συφορβοῖς καὶ βουκόλοις ἐοικότες, ἀλλ' οἴους ἄν τις ἀξιώσειε τοὺς ἐκ βασιλείου τε φύντας γένους, καὶ ἀπὸ δαιμόνων

Cato the Censor, who also lived in the days of
the Second Punic War, mentioned this lost litera-

σποράς γινέσθαι νομιζομένους, ὡς ἐν τοῖς πατρίοις ὕμνοις ὑπὸ
'Ρωμαίων ἔτι καὶ νῦν ᾄδεται.—*Dion. Hal.* i. 79. This passage
has sometimes been cited as if Dionysius had been speaking in
his own person, and had, Greek as he was, been so industrious
or so fortunate as to discover some valuable remains of that
early Latin poetry which the greatest Latin writers of his age
regretted as hopelessly lost. Such a supposition is highly
improbable; and indeed it seems clear from the context that
Dionysius, as Reiske and other editors evidently thought,
was merely quoting from Fabius Pictor. The whole passage
has the air of an extract from an ancient chronicle, and is
introduced by the words, Κόιντος μὲν Φάβιος, ὁ Πίκτωρ λεγόμενος,
τῇδε γράφει. .

Another argument may be urged which seems to deserve
consideration. The author of the passage in question mentions
a thatched hut which, in his time, stood between the summit
of Mount Palatine and the Circus. This hut, he says, was built
by Romulus, and was constantly kept in repair at the public
charge, but never in any respect embellished. Now, in the
age of Dionysius there certainly was at Rome a thatched hut,
said to have been that of Romulus. But this hut, as we learn
from Vitruvius, stood, not near the Circus, but in the Capitol.
(*Vit.* ii. 1.) If, therefore, we understand Dionysius to speak in
his own person, we can reconcile his statement with that of
Vitruvius only by supposing that there were at Rome, in the
Augustan age, two thatched huts, both believed to have been
built by Romulus, and both carefully repaired and held in high
honour. The objections to such a supposition seem to be strong.
Neither Dionysius nor Vitruvius speaks of more than one such
hut. Dio Cassius informs us that twice, during the long administration of Augustus, the hut of Romulus caught fire.
(xlviii. 43, liv. 29.) Had there been two such huts, would he
not have told us of which he spoke? An English historian
would hardly give an account of a fire at Queen's College
without saying whether it was at Queen's College, Oxford, or
at Queen's College, Cambridge. Marcus Seneca, Macrobius,

ture in his lost work on the antiquities of his country. Many ages, he said, before his time, there were ballads in praise of illustrious men; and these ballads it was the fashion for the guests at banquets to sing in turn while the piper played. 'Would,' exclaims Cicero, 'that we still had the old ballads of which Cato speaks!'*

and Conon, a Greek writer from whom Photius has made large extracts, mention only one hut of Romulus, that in the Capitol. (*M. Seneca, Contr.* i. 6.; *Macrobius, Sat.* i. 15.; *Photius, Bibl.* 186.) Ovid, Livy, Petronius, Valerius Maximus, Lucius Seneca, and St. Jerome, mention only one hut of Romulus, without specifying the site. (*Ovid. Fasti,* iii. 183.; *Liv.* v. 53.; *Petronius, Fragm.; Val. Max.* iv. 4.; *L. Seneca, Consolatio ad Helviam; D. Hieron. ad Paulinianum de Didymo.*)

The whole difficulty is removed, if we suppose that Dionysius was merely quoting Fabius Pictor. Nothing is more probable than that the cabin, which in the time of Fabius stood near the Circus, might, long before the age of Augustus, have been transported to the Capitol, as the place fittest, by reason both of its safety and of its sanctity, to contain so precious a relic.

The language of Plutarch confirms this hypothesis. He describes, with great precision, the spot where Romulus dwelt, on the slope of Mount Palatine leading to the Circus; but he says not a word implying that the dwelling was still to be seen there. Indeed, his expressions imply that it was no longer there. The evidence of Solinus is still more to the point. He, like Plutarch, describes the spot where Romulus had resided, and says expressly that the hut had been there, but that in his time it was there no longer. The site, it is certain, was well remembered; and probably retained its old name, as Charing Cross and the Haymarket have done. This is probably the explanation of the words 'casa Romuli,' in Victor's description of the Tenth Region of Rome, under Valentinian.

* Cicero refers twice to this important passage in Cato's

Valerius Maximus gives us exactly similar information, without mentioning his authority, and observes that the ancient Roman ballads were probably of more benefit to the young than all the lectures of the Athenian schools, and that to the influence of the national poetry were to be ascribed the virtues of such men as Camillus and Fabricius.*

Varro, whose authority on all questions connected with the antiquities of his country is entitled to the greatest respect, tells us that at banquets it was once the fashion for boys to sing, sometimes with and sometimes without instrumental music, ancient ballads in praise of men of former times. These young performers, he observes, were of unblemished character, a circumstance which he probably mentioned because, among the Greeks, and indeed in his time among the Romans

Antiquities:—'Gravissimus auctor in Originibus dixit Cato, morem apud majores hunc epularum fuisse, ut deinceps, qui accubarent, canerent ad tibiam clarorum virorum laudes atque virtutes. Ex quo perspicuum est, et cantus tum fuisse rescriptos vocum sonis, et carmina.'—*Tusc. Quæst.* iv. 2. Again: 'Utinam exstarent illa carmina, quæ, multis sæculis ante suam ætatem, in epulis esse cantitata a singulis convivis de clarorum virorum laudibus, in Originibus scriptum reliquit Cato.'— *Brutus*, xix.

* 'Majores natu in conviviis ad tibias egregia superiorum opera carmine comprehensa pangebant, quo ad ea imitanda juventutem alacriorem redderent. . . . Quas Athenas, quam scholam, quæ alienigena studia huic domesticæ disciplinæ prætulerim? Inde oriebantur Camilli, Scipiones, Fabricii, Marcelli, Fabii.'—*Val. Max.* ii. 1.

also, the morals of singing boys were in no high repute.*

The testimony of Horace, though given incidentally, confirms the statements of Cato, Valerius Maximus, and Varro. The poet predicts that, under the peaceful administration of Augustus, the Romans will, over their full goblets, sing to the pipe, after the fashion of their fathers, the deeds of brave captains, and the ancient legends touching the origin of the city.†

The proposition, then, that Rome had ballad-poetry is not merely in itself highly probable, but is fully proved by direct evidence of the greatest weight.

This proposition being established, it becomes easy to understand why the early history of the city is unlike almost everything else in Latin literature, native where almost everything else is borrowed, imaginative where almost everything

---

* ' In conviviis pueri modesti ut cantarent carmina antiqua, in quibus laudes erant majorum, et assa voce, et cum tibicine.'
Nonius, *Assa voce pro sola.*

    † 'Nosque et profestis lucibus et sacris,
      Inter jocosi munera Liberi,
        Cum prole matronisque nostris,
        Rite Deos prius apprecati,
      Virtute functos, more patrum, duces,
      Lydis remixto carmine tibiis,
        Trojamque, et Anchisen, et almæ
        Progeniem Veneris canemus.'

                              *Carm.* iv. 15.

else is prosaic. We can scarcely hesitate to pronounce that the magnificent, pathetic, and truly
national legends, which present so striking a
contrast to all that surrounds them, are broken
and defaced fragments of that early poetry which,
even in the age of Cato the Censor, had become
antiquated, and of which Tully had never heard
a line.

That this poetry should have been suffered to
perish will not appear strange when we consider
how complete was the triumph of the Greek
genius over the public mind of Italy. It is
probable that, at an early period, Homer and
Herodotus furnished some hints to the Latin
minstrels:* but it was not till after the war with
Pyrrhus that the poetry of Rome began to put
off its old Ausonian character. The transforma-
tion was soon consummated. The conquered,
says Horace, led captive the conquerors. It was
precisely at the time at which the Roman people
rose to unrivalled political ascendency that they
stooped to pass under the intellectual yoke. It was
precisely at the time at which the sceptre departed
from Greece that the empire of her language and
of her arts became universal and despotic. The
revolution indeed was not effected without a
struggle. Nævius seems to have been the last
of the ancient line of poets. Ennius was the

* See the Preface to the Lay of the Battle of Regillus.

founder of a new dynasty. Nævius celebrated
the First Punic War in Saturnian verse, the old
national verse of Italy.* Ennius sang the Second

* Cicero speaks highly in more than one place of this poem
of Nævius; Ennius sneered at it, and stole from it.

As to the Saturnian measure, see Hermann's *Elementa
Doctrinæ Metricæ*, iii. 9.

The Saturnian line, according to the grammarians, consisted
of two parts. The first was a catalectic dimeter iambic; the
second was composed of three trochees. But the licence taken
by the early Latin poets seems to have been almost boundless.
The most perfect Saturnian line which has been preserved was
the work, not of a professional artist, but of an amateur:

'Dabunt malum Metelli Nævio poetæ.'

There has been much difference of opinion among learned
men respecting the history of this measure. That it is the
same with a Greek measure used by Archilochus is in-
disputable. (*Bentley, Phalaris*, xi.) But in spite of the authority of Terentianus Maurus, and of the still higher authority
of Bentley, we may venture to doubt whether the coincidence
was not fortuitous. We constantly find the same rude and
simple numbers in different countries, under circumstances
which make it impossible to suspect that there has been
imitation on either side. Bishop Heber heard the children of a
village in Bengal singing 'Radha, Radha,' to the tune of 'My
boy Billy.' Neither the Castilian nor the German minstrels of
the middle ages owed anything to Paros or to ancient Rome.
Yet both the poem of the Cid and the poem of the Nibelungs
contain many Saturnian verses; as,—

'Estas nuevas á mio Cid eran venidas.'

'Á mi lo dicen; á ti dan las orejadas.'

'Man möhte michel wunder von Sifride sagen.'

'Wa ich den Künic vinde daz sol man mir sagen.'

Indeed, there cannot be a more perfect Saturnian line than one
which is sung in every English nursery—

'The queen was in her parlour eating bread and honey;'

Punic War in numbers borrowed from the Iliad.
The elder poet, in the epitaph which he wrote

yet the author of this line, we may be assured, borrowed
nothing from either Nævius or Archilochus.

On the other hand, it is by no means improbable that, two
or three hundred years before the time of Ennius, some Latin
minstrel may have visited Sybaris or Crotona, may have heard
some verses of Archilochus sung, may have been pleased with
the metre, and may have introduced it at Rome. Thus much
is certain, that the Saturnian measure, if not a native of Italy,
was at least so early and so completely naturalised there that
its foreign origin was forgotten.

Bentley says indeed that the Saturnian measure was first
brought from Greece into Italy by Nævius. But this is
merely *obiter dictum*, to use a phrase common in our courts of
law, and would not have been deliberately maintained by that
incomparable critic, whose memory is held in reverence by all
lovers of learning. The arguments which might be brought
against Bentley's assertion—for it is mere assertion, supported
by no evidence—are innumerable. A few will suffice.

1. Bentley's assertion is opposed to the testimony of Ennius.
Ennius sneered at Nævius for writing on the First Punic War
in verses such as the old Italian Bards used before Greek literature had been studied. Now the poem of Nævius was in
Saturnian verse. Is it possible that Ennius could have used
such expressions, if the Saturnian verse had been just imported
from Greece for the first time?

2. Bentley's assertion is opposed to the testimony of Horace.
'When Greece,' says Horace, 'introduced her arts into our un-
civilised country, those rugged Saturnian numbers passed away.'
Would Horace have said this, if the Saturnian numbers had
been imported from Greece just before the hexameter?

3. Bentley's assertion is opposed to the testimony of Festus
and of Aurelius Victor, both of whom positively say that the
most ancient prophecies attributed to the Fauns were in Saturnian verse.

4. Bentley's assertion is opposed to the testimony of Teren-

for himself, and which is a fine specimen of the
early Roman diction and versification, plaintively
boasted that the Latin language had died with
him.* Thus what to Horace appeared to be the
first faint dawn of Roman literature, appeared to
Nævius to be its hopeless setting. In truth, one
literature was setting, and another dawning.

The victory of the foreign taste was decisive :
and indeed we can hardly blame the Romans for
turning away with contempt from the rude lays
which had delighted their fathers, and giving
their whole admiration to the immortal productions of Greece. The national romances, neglected
by the great and the refined whose education had
been finished at Rhodes or Athens, continued, it
may be supposed, during some generations, to

tianus Maurus, to whom he has himself appealed. Terentianus
Maurus does indeed say that the Saturnian measure, though
believed by the Romans from a very early period ('credidit
vetustas') to be of Italian invention, was really borrowed from
the Greeks. But Terentianus Maurus does not say that it was
first borrowed by Nævius. Nay, the expressions used by Terentianus Maurus clearly imply the contrary : for how could
the Romans have believed, from a very early period, that this
measure was the indigenous production of Latium, if it was
really brought over from Greece in an age of intelligence and
liberal curiosity, in the age which gave birth to Ennius, Plautus,
Cato the Censor, and other distinguished writers ? If Bentley's
assertion were correct, there could have been no more doubt at
Rome about the Greek origin of the Saturnian measure than
about the Greek origin of hexameters or Sapphics.

  * Aulus Gellius, Noctes Atticæ, i. 24.

delight the vulgar. While Virgil, in hexameters of exquisite modulation, described the sports of rustics, those rustics were still singing their wild Saturnian ballads.* It is not improbable that, at the time when Cicero lamented the irreparable loss of the poems mentioned by Cato, a search among the nooks of the Apennines, as active as the search which Sir Walter Scott made among the descendants of the mosstroopers of Liddesdale, might have brought to light many fine remains of ancient minstrelsy. No such search was made. The Latin ballads perished for ever. Yet discerning critics have thought that they could still perceive in the early history of Rome numerous fragments of this lost poetry, as the traveller on classic ground sometimes finds, built into the heavy wall of a fort or convent, a pillar rich with acanthus leaves, or a frieze where the Amazons and Bacchanals seem to live. The theatres and temples of the Greek and the Roman were degraded into the quarries of the Turk and the Goth. Even so did the ancient Saturnian poetry become the quarry in which a crowd of orators and annalists found the materials for their prose.

It is not difficult to trace the process by which the old songs were transmuted into the form which they now wear. Funeral panegyric and chronicle appear to have been the intermediate links which

* See Servius, in Georg. ii. 385.

connected the lost ballads with the histories
now extant. From a very early period it was the
usage that an oration should be pronounced over
the remains of a noble Roman. The orator, as
we learn from Polybius, was expected, on such
an occasion, to recapitulate all the services which
the ancestors of the deceased had, from the earliest
time, rendered to the commonwealth. There
can be little doubt that the speaker on whom
this duty was imposed would make use of all the
stories suited to his purpose which were to be
found in the popular lays. There can be as little
doubt that the family of an eminent man would
preserve a copy of the speech which had been
pronounced over his corpse. The compilers of
the early chronicles would have recourse to these
speeches; and the great historians of a later
period would have recourse to the chronicles.

It may be worth while to select a particular
story, and to trace its probable progress through
these stages. The description of the migration
of the Fabian house to Cremera is one of the
finest of the many fine passages which lie thick
in the earlier books of Livy. The Consul, clad in
his military garb, stands in the vestibule of his
house, marshalling his clan, three hundred and six
fighting men, all of the same proud patrician
blood, all worthy to be attended by the fasces, and
to command the legions. A sad and anxious

retinue of friends accompanies the adventurers
through the streets; but the voice of lamentation
is drowned by the shouts of admiring thousands.
As the procession passes the Capitol, prayers and
vows are poured forth, but in vain. The devoted
band, leaving Janus on the right, marches to its
doom through the Gate of Evil Luck. After achiev-
ing high deeds of valour against overwhelming
numbers, all perish save one child, the stock from
which the great Fabian race was destined again to
spring for the safety and glory of the commonwealth. That this fine romance, the details of
which are so full of poetical truth, and so utterly
destitute of all show of historical truth, came
originally from some lay which had often been
sung with great applause at banquets, is in the
highest degree probable. Nor is it difficult to
imagine a mode in which the transmission might
have taken place. The celebrated Quintus Fabius
Maximus, who died about twenty years before the
First Punic War, and more than forty years before
Ennius was born, is said to have been interred
with extraordinary pomp. In the eulogy pronounced over his body all the great exploits of
his ancestors were doubtless recounted and exaggerated. If there were then extant songs which
gave a vivid and touching description of an event,
the saddest and the most glorious in the long
history of the Fabian house, nothing could be

more natural than that the panegyrist should
borrow from such songs their finest touches, in
order to adorn his speech. A few generations
later the songs would perhaps be forgotten, or
remembered only by shepherds and vine-dressers.
But the speech would certainly be preserved in
the archives of the Fabian nobles. Fabius Pictor
would be well acquainted with a document so
interesting to his personal feelings, and would
insert large extracts from it in his rude chronicle.
That chronicle, as we know, was the oldest to
which Livy had access. Livy would at a glance
distinguish the bold strokes of the forgotten poet
from the dull and feeble narrative by which they
were surrounded, would retouch them with a
delicate and powerful pencil, and would make
them immortal.

That this might happen at Rome can scarcely be
doubted; for something very like this has happened
in several countries, and, among others, in our
own. Perhaps the theory of Perizonius cannot
be better illustrated than by showing that what
he supposes to have taken place in ancient times
has, beyond all doubt, taken place in modern
times.

'History,' says Hume with the utmost gravity,
'has preserved some instances of Edgar's amours,
from which, as from a specimen, we may form a
conjecture of the rest.' He then tells very agree-

ably the stories of Elfleda and Elfrida, two stories which have a most suspicious air of romance, and which, indeed, greatly resemble, in their general character, some of the legends of early Rome. He cites, as his authority for these two tales, the chronicle of William of Malmesbury, who lived in the time of King Stephen. The great majority of readers suppose that the device by which Elfrida was substituted for her young mistress, the artifice by which Athelwold obtained the hand of Elfrida, the detection of that artifice, the hunting party, and the vengeance of the amorous king, are things about which there is no more doubt than about the execution of Anne Boleyn, or the slitting of Sir John Coventry's nose. But when we turn to William of Malmesbury, we find that Hume, in his eagerness to relate these pleasant fables, has overlooked one very important circumstance. William does indeed tell both the stories; but he gives us distinct notice that he does not warrant their truth, and that they rest on no better authority than that of ballads.*

Such is the way in which these two well-known tales have been handed down. They originally appeared in a poetical form. They found their

---

\* 'Infamias quas post dicam magis resperserunt cantilenæ.' Edgar appears to have been most mercilessly treated in the Anglo-Saxon ballads. He was the favourite of the monks; and the monks and the minstrels were at deadly feud.

way from ballads into an old chronicle. The ballads perished; the chronicle remained. A great historian, some centuries after the ballads had been altogether forgotten, consulted the chronicle. He was struck by the lively colouring of these ancient fictions: he transferred them to his pages; and thus we find inserted, as unquestionable facts, in a narrative which is likely to last as long as the English tongue, the inventions of some minstrel whose works were probably never committed to writing, whose name is buried in oblivion, and whose dialect has become obsolete. It must, then, be admitted to be possible, or rather highly probable, that the stories of Romulus and Remus, and of the Horatii and Curiatii, may have had a similar origin.

Castilian literature will furnish us with another parallel case. Mariana, the classical historian of Spain, tells the story of the ill-starred marriage which the King Don Alonso brought about between the heirs of Carrion and the two daughters of the Cid. The Cid bestowed a princely dower on his sons-in-law. But the young men were base and proud, cowardly and cruel. They were tried in danger, and found wanting. They fled before the Moors, and once, when a lion broke out of his den, they ran and crouched in an unseemly hiding-place. They knew that they were despised, and took counsel how they might be avenged. They parted from their father-in-law with many signs of love, and set forth on a journey with Doña Elvira and Doña Sol. In a solitary place the bridegrooms seized their brides, stripped them, scourged them, and departed, leaving them for dead. But one of the house of Bivar, suspecting foul play, had followed the travellers in disguise. The ladies were brought back safe to the house of their father. Complaint was made to the king. It was adjudged by the Cortes that the dower given by the Cid should be returned, and that the heirs of Carrion together with one of their kindred should do battle against three knights of the party of the Cid. The guilty youths would have declined the combat; but all their shifts were vain. They were vanquished in the lists, and for ever disgraced, while their injured wives were sought in marriage by great princes.*

Some Spanish writers have laboured to show, by an examination of dates and circumstances, that this story is untrue. Such confutation was surely not needed; for the narrative is on the face of it a romance. How it found its way into Mariana's history is quite clear. He acknowledges his obligations to the ancient chronicles; and had doubtless before him the ' Cronica del famoso Cavallero Cid Ruy Diez Campeador,' which

* Mariana, lib. x. cap. 4.

had been printed as early as the year 1552. He
little suspected that all the most striking passages
in this chronicle were copied from a poem of the
twelfth century, a poem of which the language
and versification had long been obsolete, but
which glowed with no common portion of the fire
of the Iliad. Yet such was the fact. More than
a century and a half after the death of Mariana,
this venerable ballad, of which one imperfect copy
on parchment, four hundred years old, had been
preserved at Bivar, was for the first time printed.
Then it was found that every interesting circumstance of the story of the heirs of Carrion was
derived by the eloquent Jesuit from a song of
which he had never heard, and which was composed by a minstrel whose very name had long
been forgotten.*

Such, or nearly such, appears to have been the
process by which the lost ballad-poetry of Rome
was transformed into history. To reverse that
process, to transform some portions of early Roman
history back into the poetry out of which they
were made, is the object of this work.

In the following poems the author speaks, not
in his own person, but in the persons of ancient

* See the account which Sanchez gives of the Bivar manuscript in the first volume of the *Coleccion de Poesias Castella-
nas anteriores al Siglo XV.* Part of the story of the lords of
Carrion, in the poem of the Cid, has been translated by Mr.
Frere in a manner above all praise.

minstrels who know only what a Roman citizen, born three or four hundred years before the Christian æra, may be supposed to have known, and who are in nowise above the passions and prejudices of their age and nation. To these imaginary poets must be ascribed some blunders which are so obvious that it is unnecessary to point them out. The real blunder would have been to represent these old poets as deeply versed in general history, and studious of chronological accuracy. To them must also be attributed the illiberal sneers at the Greeks, the furious party-spirit, the contempt for the arts of peace, the love of war for its own sake, the ungenerous exultation over the vanquished, which the reader will sometimes observe. To portray a Roman of the age of Camillus or Curius as superior to national antipathies, as mourning over the devastation and slaughter by which empire and triumphs were to be won, as looking on human suffering with the sympathy of Howard, or as treating conquered enemies with the delicacy of the Black Prince, would be to violate all dramatic propriety. The old Romans had some great virtues, fortitude, temperance, veracity, spirit to resist oppression, respect for legitimate authority, fidelity in the observing of contracts, disinterestedness, ardent patriotism; but Christian charity and chivalrous generosity were alike unknown to them.

It would have been obviously improper to mimic the manner of any particular age or country. Something has been borrowed, however, from our own old ballads, and more from Sir Walter Scott, the great restorer of our ballad-poetry. To the Iliad still greater obligations are due; and those obligations have been contracted with the less hesitation, because there is reason to believe that some of the old Latin minstrels really had recourse to that inexhaustible store of poetical images.

It would have been easy to swell this little volume to a very considerable bulk, by appending notes filled with quotations; but to a learned reader such notes are not necessary; for an unlearned reader they would have little interest; and the judgment passed both by the learned and by the unlearned on a work of the imagination will always depend much more on the general character and spirit of such a work than on minute details.

# HORATIUS.

a

# HORATIUS.

THERE can be little doubt that among those parts of early Roman history which had a poetical origin was the legend of Horatius Cocles. We have several versions of the story, and these versions differ from each other in points of no small importance. Polybius, there is reason to believe, heard the tale recited over the remains of some Consul or Prætor descended from the old Horatian patricians; for he introduces it as a specimen of the narratives with which the Romans were in the habit of embellishing their funeral oratory. It is remarkable that, according to him, Horatius defended the bridge alone, and perished in the waters. According to the chronicles which Livy and Dionysius followed, Horatius had two companions, swam safe to shore, and was loaded with honours and rewards.

These discrepancies are easily explained. Our own literature, indeed, will furnish an exact parallel to what may have taken place at Rome. It is highly probable that the memory of the war of Porsena was preserved by compositions much resembling the two ballads which stand first in the *Relics of Ancient English Poetry*. In both those ballads the English, commanded by the Percy, fight with the Scots, commanded by the Douglas. In one of the ballads the Douglas is killed by a nameless English archer, and the Percy by a Scottish spearman: in the other, the Percy slays the Douglas in single combat, and is himself made prisoner. In the former, Sir Hugh Montgomery is shot through the heart by a Northumbrian bowman: in the latter he is taken, and exchanged for the Percy. Yet both the ballads relate to the same event, and that an event which probably took place within the memory of persons who were alive when both the ballads were made. One of the minstrels says:

> ‘Old men that knowen the grounde well yenoughe
> Call it the battell of Otterburn:
> At Otterburn began this spurne
> Upon a monnyn day.
> Ther was the doughte Doglas slean:
> The Perse never went away.’

The other poet sums up the event in the following lines:

> ‘Thys frayo bygan at Otterborne
> Bytwene the nyghte and the day:
> Ther the Dowglas lost hys lyfe,
> And the Percy was lede away.’

It is by no means unlikely that there were two old Roman lays about the defence of the bridge; and that, while the story which Livy has transmitted to us was preferred by the multitude, the other, which ascribed the whole glory to Horatius alone, may have been the favourite with the Horatian house.

The following ballad is supposed to have been made about a hundred and twenty years after the war which it celebrates, and just before the taking of Rome by the Gauls. The author seems to have been an honest citizen, proud of the military glory of his country, sick of the disputes of factions, and much given to pining after good old times which had never really existed. The allusion, however, to the partial manner in which the public lands were allotted could proceed only from a plebeian; and the allusion to the fraudulent sale of spoils marks the date of the poem, and shows that the poet shared in the general discontent with which the proceedings of Camillus, after the taking of Veii, were regarded.

The penultimate syllable of the name Porsena has been shortened in spite of the authority of Niebuhr, who pronounces, without assigning any ground for his opinion, that Martial was guilty of a decided blunder in the line,

'Hanc spectare manum Porsena non potuit.'

It is not easy to understand how any modern

scholar, whatever his attainments may be,—and those of Niebuhr were undoubtedly immense,—can venture to pronounce that Martial did not know the quantity of a word which he must have uttered and heard uttered a hundred times before he left school. Niebuhr seems also to have forgotten that Martial has fellow-culprits to keep him in countenance. Horace has committed the same decided blunder; for he gives us, as a pure iambic line,

'Minacis aut Etrusca Porsenæ manus.'

Silius Italicus has repeatedly offended in the same way, as when he says,

'Cernitur effugiens ardentem Porsena dextram:'

and again,

'Clusinum vulgus, cum, Porsena magne, jubebas.'

A modern writer may be content to err in such company.

Niebuhr's supposition that each of the three defenders of the bridge was the representative of one of the three patrician tribes is both ingenious and probable, and has been adopted in the following poem.

# HORATIUS.

A LAY MADE ABOUT THE YEAR OF THE CITY
CCCLI.

I.

Lars Porsena of Clusium
  By the Nine Gods he swore
That the great house of Tarquin
  Should suffer wrong no more.
By the Nine Gods he swore it,
  And named a trysting day,
And bade his messengers ride forth,
East and west and south and north,
  To summon his array.

II.

East and west and south and north
  The messengers ride fast,
And tower and town and cottage
  Have heard the trumpet's blast.
Shame on the false Etruscan
  Who lingers in his home,
When Porsena of Clusium
  Is on the march for Rome.

III.

The horsemen and the footmen
  Are pouring in amain
From many a stately market-place;
  From many a fruitful plain;
From many a lonely hamlet,
  Which, hid by beech and pine,
Like an eagle's nest, hangs on the crest
  Of purple Apennine;


IV.


From lordly Volaterræ,
  Where scowls the far-famed hold
Piled by the hands of giants
  For godlike kings of old;
From seagirt Populonia,
  Whose sentinels descry
Sardinia's snowy mountain-tops
  Fringing the southern sky;


V.


From the proud mart of Pisæ,
  Queen of the western waves,
Where ride Massilia's triremes
  Heavy with fair-haired slaves;
From where sweet Clanis wanders
  Through corn and vines and flowers;
From where Cortona lifts to heaven
  Her diadem of towers.

VI.

Tall are the oaks whose acorns
  Drop in dark Auser's rill;
Fat are the stags that champ the boughs
  Of the Ciminian hill;
Beyond all streams Clitumnus
  Is to the herdsman dear;
Best of all pools the fowler loves
  The great Volsinian mere.


VII.

But now no stroke of woodman
  Is heard by Auser's rill;
No hunter tracks the stag's green path
  Up the Ciminian hill;
Unwatched along Clitumnus
  Grazes the milk-white steer;
Unharmed the water fowl may dip
  In the Volsinian mere.


VIII.

The harvests of Arretium,
  This year, old men shall reap,
This year, young boys in Umbro
  Shall plunge the struggling sheep;
And in the vats of Luna,
  This year, the must shall foam
Round the white feet of laughing girls
  Whose sires have marched to Rome.

### IX.

There be thirty chosen prophets,
  The wisest of the land,
Who alway by Lars Porsena
  Both morn and evening stand :
Evening and morn the Thirty
  Have turned the verses o'er,
Traced from the right on linen white
  By mighty seers of yore.

### X.

And with one voice the Thirty
  Have their glad answer given :
' Go forth, go forth, Lars Porsena ;
  Go forth, beloved of Heaven;
Go, and return in glory
  To Clusium's royal dome ;
And hang round Nurscia's altars
  The golden shields of Rome.'

### XI.

And now hath every city
  Sent up her tale of men ;
The foot are fourscore thousand,
  The horse are thousands ten
Before the gates of Sutrium
  Is met the great array.
A proud man was Lars Porsena
  Upon the trysting day.

### XII.

For all the Etruscan armies
  Were ranged beneath his eye,
And many a banished Roman,
  And many a stout ally;
And with a mighty following
  To join the muster came
The Tusculan Mamilius,
  Prince of the Latian name.

### XIII.

But by the yellow Tiber
  Was tumult and affright:
From all the spacious champaign
  To Rome men took their flight.
A mile around the city,
  The throng stopped up the ways;
A fearful sight it was to see
  Through two long nights and days.

### XIV.

For aged folks on crutches,
  And women great with child,
And mothers sobbing over babes
  That clung to them and smiled.
And sick men borne in litters
  High on the necks of slaves,
And troops of sun-burned husbandmen
  With reaping-hooks and staves,

### XV.

And droves of mules and asses
　　Laden with skins of wine,
And endless flocks of goats and sheep,
　　And endless herds of kine,
And endless trains of waggons
　　That creaked beneath the weight
Of corn-sacks and of household goods,
　　Choked every roaring gate.

### XVI.

Now, from the rock Tarpeian,
　　Could the wan burghers spy
The line of blazing villages
　　Red in the midnight sky.
The Fathers of the City,
　　They sat all night and day,
For every hour some horseman came
　　With tidings of dismay.

### XVII.

To eastward and to westward
　　Have spread the Tuscan bands;
Nor house, nor fence, nor dovecote
　　In Crustumerium stands.
Verbenna down to Ostia
　　Hath wasted all the plain;
Astur hath stormed Janiculum,
　　And the stout guards are slain.

### XVIII.

I wis, in all the Senate,
  There was no heart so bold,
But sore it ached, and fast it beat,
  When that ill news was told.
Forthwith up rose the Consul,
  Up rose the Fathers all ;
In haste they girded up their gowns,
  And hied them to the wall.

### XIX.

They held a council standing
  Before the River-Gate ;
Short time was there, ye well may guess,
  For musing or debate.
Out spake the Consul roundly :
  ' The bridge must straight go down ;
For, since Janiculum is lost,
  Nought else can save the town.'

### XX.

Just then a scout came flying,
  All wild with haste and fear :
' To arms ! to arms ! Sir Consul :
  Lars Porsena is here.'
On the low hills to westward
  The Consul fixed his eye,
And saw the swarthy storm of dust
  Rise fast along the sky.

## XXI.

And nearer fast and nearer
　Doth the red whirlwind come ;
And louder still and still more loud,
From underneath that rolling cloud,
Is heard the trumpet's war-note proud,
　The trampling, and the hum.
And plainly and more plainly
　Now through the gloom appears,
Far to left and far to right,
In broken gleams of dark-blue light,
The long array of helmets bright,
　The long array of spears.

## XXII.

And plainly and more plainly,
　Above that glimmering line,
Now might ye see the banners
　Of twelve fair cities shine ;
But the banner of proud Clusium
　Was highest of them all,
The terror of the Umbrian,
　The terror of the Gaul.

## XXIII.

And plainly and more plainly
　Now might the burghers know,
By port and vest, by horse and crest,
　Each warlike Lucumo.

There Cilnius of Arretium
  On his fleet roan was seen;
And Astur of the four-fold shield,
Girt with the brand none else may wield,
Tolumnius with the belt of gold,
And dark Verbenna from the hold
  By reedy Thrasymene.

## XXIV.

Fast by the royal standard,
  O'erlooking all the war,
Lars Porsena of Clusium
  Sat in his ivory car.
By the right wheel rode Mamilius,
  Prince of the Latian name;
And by the left false Sextus,
  That wrought the deed of shame.

## XXV.

But when the face of Sextus
  Was seen among the foes,
A yell that rent the firmament
  From all the town arose.
On the house-tops was no woman
  But spat towards him and hissed,
No child but screamed out curses,
  And shook its little fist.

XXVI.

But the Consul's brow was sad,
　And the Consul's speech was low,
And darkly looked he at the wall,
　And darkly at the foe.
'Their van will be upon us
　Before the bridge goes down;
And if they once may win the bridge,
　What hope to save the town?'

XXVII.

Then out spake brave Horatius,
　The Captain of the Gate:
'To every man upon this earth
　Death cometh soon or late.
And how can man die better
　Than facing fearful odds,
For the ashes of his fathers,
　And the temples of his Gods,

XXVIII.

'And for the tender mother
　Who dandled him to rest,
And for the wife who nurses
　His baby at her breast,
And for the holy maidens
　Who feed the eternal flame,
To save them from false Sextus
　That wrought the deed of shame?

### XXIX.

' How down the bridge, Sir Consul,
  With all the speed ye may;
I, with two more to help me,
  Will hold the foe in play.
In yon strait path a thousand
  May well be stopped by three.
Now who will stand on either hand,
  And keep the bridge with me ? '

### XXX.

Then out spake Spurius Lartius;
  A Ramnian proud was he:
' Lo, I will stand at thy right hand,
  And keep tho bridge with thee.'
And out spake strong Herminius;
  Of Titian blood was he:
' I will abide on thy left side,
  And keep the bridge with thee.'

### XXXI.

' Horatius,' quoth the Consul,
  ' As thou sayest, so let it be.'
And straight against that great array
  Forth went the dauntless Three.
For Romans in Rome's quarrel
  Spared neither land nor gold,
Nor son nor wife, nor limb nor life,
  In the brave days of old.

D

### XXXII.

Then none was for a party;
  Then all were for the state;
Then the great man helped the poor,
  And the poor man loved the great:
Then lands were fairly portioned;
  Then spoils were fairly sold:
The Romans were like brothers
  In the brave days of old.

### XXXIII.

Now Roman is to Roman
  More hateful than a foe,
And the Tribunes beard the high,
  And the Fathers grind the low.
As we wax hot in faction,
  In battle we wax cold:
Wherefore men fight not as they fought
  In the brave days of old.

### XXXIV.

Now while the Three were tightening
  Their harness on their backs,
The Consul was the foremost man
  To take in hand an axe:
And Fathers mixed with Commons
  Seized hatchet, bar, and crow,
And smote upon the planks above,
  And loosed the props below.

### XXXV.

Meanwhile the Tuscan army,
  Right glorious to behold,
Came flashing back the noonday light,
Rank behind rank, like surges bright
  Of a broad sea of gold.
Four hundred trumpets sounded
  A peal of warlike glee,
As that great host, with measured tread,
And spears advanced, and ensigns spread,
Rolled slowly towards the bridge's head,
  Where stood the dauntless Three.


### XXXVI.

The Three stood calm and silent,
  And looked upon the foes,
And a great shout of laughter
  From all the vanguard rose :
And forth three chiefs came spurring
  Before that deep array ;
To earth they sprang, their swords they drew,
And lifted high their shields, and flew
  To win the narrow way ;


### XXXVII.

Aunus from green Tifernum,
  Lord of the Hill of Vines ;
And Seius, whose eight hundred slaves
  Sicken in Ilva's mines ;

And Picus, long to Clusium
  Vassal in peace and war,
Who led to fight his Umbrian powers
From that grey crag where, girt with towers,
The fortress of Nequinum lowers
  O'er the pale waves of Nar.


### XXXVIII.

Stout Lartius hurled down Aunus
  Into the stream beneath:
Herminius struck at Seius,
  And clove him to the teeth:
At Picus brave Horatius
  Darted one fiery thrust;
And the proud Umbrian's gilded arms
  Clashed in the bloody dust.


### XXXIX.

Then Ocnus of Falerii
  Rushed on the Roman Three;
And Lausulus of Urgo,
  The rover of the sea;
And Aruns of Volsinium,
  Who slew the great wild boar,
The great wild boar that had his den
Amidst the reeds of Cosa's fen,
And wasted fields, and slaughtered men,
  Along Albinia's shore.

### XL.

Herminius smote down Aruns :
    Lartius laid Ocnus low :
Right to the heart of Lausulus
    Horatius sent a blow.
' Lie there,' he cried, ' fell pirate !
    No more, aghast and pale,
From Ostia's walls the crowd shall mark
The track of thy destroying bark.
No more Campania's hinds shall fly
To woods and caverns when they spy
    Thy thrice accursed sail.'

### XLI.

But now no sound of laughter
    Was heard among the foes.
A wild and wrathful clamour
    From all the vanguard rose.
Six spears' lengths from the entrance
    Halted that deep array,
And for a space no man came forth
    To win the narrow way.

### XLII.

But hark ! the cry is Astur :
    And lo ! the ranks divide ;

And the great Lord of Luna
  Comes with his stately stride.
Upon his ample shoulders
  Clangs loud the fourfold shield,
And in his hand he shakes the brand
  Which none but he can wield.


### XLIII.

He smiled on those bold Romans
  A smile serene and high;
He eyed the flinching Tuscans,
  And scorn was in his eye.
Quoth he, 'The she-wolf's litter
  Stand savagely at bay:
But will ye dare to follow,
  If Astur clears the way?'


### XLIV.

Then, whirling up his broadsword
  With both hands to the height,
He rushed against Horatius,
  And smote with all his might.
With shield and blade Horatius
  Right deftly turned the blow.
The blow, though turned, came yet too nigh;
It missed his helm, but gashed his thigh:
The Tuscans raised a joyful cry
  To see the red blood flow.

### XLV.

He reeled, and on Herminius
　He leaned one breathing-space;
Then, like a wild cat mad with wounds,
　Sprang right at Astur's face.
Through teeth, and skull, and helmet
　So fierce a thrust he sped,
The good sword stood a hand-breadth out
　Behind the Tuscan's head.

### XLVI.

And the great Lord of Luna
　Fell at that deadly stroke,
As falls on Mount Alvernus
　A thunder-smitten oak.
Far o'er the crashing forest
　The giant arms lie spread;
And the pale augurs, muttering low,
　Gaze on the blasted head.

### XLVII.

On Astur's throat Horatius
　Right firmly pressed his heel,
And thrice and four times tugged amain,
　Ere he wrenched out the steel.
'And see,' he cried, 'the welcome,
　Fair guests, that waits you here!
What noble Lucumo comes next
　To taste our Roman cheer?'

### XLVIII.

But at his haughty challenge
  A sullen murmur ran,
Mingled of wrath, and shame, and dread,
  Along that glittering van.
There lacked not men of prowess,
  Nor men of lordly race;
For all Etruria's noblest
  Were round the fatal place.

### XLIX.

But all Etruria's noblest
  Felt their hearts sink to see
On the earth the bloody corpses,
  In the path the dauntless Three:
And, from the ghastly entrance
  Where those bold Romans stood,
All shrank, like boys who unaware,
Ranging the woods to start a hare,
Come to the mouth of the dark lair
Where, growling low, a fierce old bear
  Lies amidst bones and blood.

### L.

Was none who would be foremost
  To lead such dire attack:
But those behind cried 'Forward!'
  And those before cried 'Back!'
And backward now and forward
  Wavers the deep array;

And on the tossing sea of steel,
To and fro the standards reel;
And the victorious trumpet-peal
    Dies fitfully away.

LI.

Yet one man for one moment
    Stood out before the crowd;
Well known was he to all the Three,
    And they gave him greeting loud,
'Now welcome, welcome, Sextus!
    Now welcome to thy home!
Why dost thou stay, and turn away?
    Here lies the road to Rome.'

LII.

Thrice looked he at the city;
    Thrice looked he at the dead;
And thrice came on in fury,
    And thrice turned back in dread:
And, white with fear and hatred,
    Scowled at the narrow way
Where, wallowing in a pool of blood,
    The bravest Tuscans lay.

LIII.

But meanwhile axe and lever
    Have manfully been plied;
And now the bridge hangs tottering
    Above the boiling tide.

'Come back, come back, Horatius!'
  Loud cried the Fathers all.
'Back, Lartius! back, Herminius!
  Back, ere the ruin fall!'

### LIV.

Back darted Spurius Lartius;
  Herminius darted back:
And, as they passed, beneath their feet
  They felt the timbers crack.
But when they turned their faces,
  And on the farther shore
Saw brave Horatius stand alone,
  They would have crossed once more.

### LV.

But with a crash like thunder
  Fell every loosened beam,
And, like a dam, the mighty wreck
  Lay right athwart the stream:
And a long shout of triumph
  Rose from the walls of Rome,
As to the highest turret-tops
  Was splashed the yellow foam.

### LVI.

And, like a horse unbroken
  When first he feels the rein,
The furious river struggled hard,
  And tossed his tawny mane,

And burst the curb, and bounded,
   Rejoicing to be free,
And whirling down, in fierce career,
Battlement, and plank, and pier,
   Rushed headlong to the sea.


### LVII.

Alone stood brave Horatius,
   But constant still in mind;
Thrice thirty thousand foes before,
   And the broad flood behind.
'Down with him!' cried false Sextus,
   With a smile on his pale face.
'Now yield thee,' cried Lars Porsena,
   'Now yield thee to our grace.'


### LVIII.

Round turned he, as not deigning
   Those craven ranks to see;
Nought spake he to Lars Porsena,
   To Sextus nought spake he;
But he saw on Palatinus
   The white porch of his home;
And he spake to the noble river
   That rolls by the towers of Rome.


### LIX.

'Oh, Tiber! father Tiber!
   To whom the Romans pray,

A Roman's life, a Roman's arms,
  Take thou in charge this day!'
So he spake, and speaking sheathed
  The good sword by his side,
And with his harness on his back,
  Plunged headlong in the tide.


LX.


No sound of joy or sorrow
  Was heard from either bank;
But friends and foes in dumb surprise,
With parted lips and straining eyes,
  Stood gazing where he sank;
And when above the surges
  They saw his crest appear,
All Rome sent forth a rapturous cry,
And even the ranks of Tuscany
  Could scarce forbear to cheer.


LXI.


But fiercely ran the current,
  Swollen high by months of rain:
And fast his blood was flowing;
  And he was sore in pain,
And heavy with his armour,
  And spent with changing blows:
And oft they thought him sinking,
  But still again he rose.

## LXII.

Never, I ween, did swimmer,
  In such an evil case,
Struggle through such a raging flood
  Safe to the landing place:
But his limbs were borne up bravely
  By the brave heart within,
And our good father Tiber
  Bore bravely up his chin.*

## LXIII.

'Curse on him!' quoth false Sextus;
  'Will not the villain drown?
But for this stay, ere close of day
  We should have sacked the town!'
'Heaven help him!' quoth Lars Porsena,
  'And bring him safe to shore;
For such a gallant feat of arms
  Was never seen before.'

---

\* 'Our ladye bare upp her chinne.'
              *Ballad of Childe Waters.*

'Never heavier man and horse
Stemmed a midnight torrent's force;
  *    *    *    *    *    *
Yet, through good heart and our Lady's grace,
At length he gained the landing place.'
              *Lay of the Last Minstrel*, I.

### LXIV.

And now he feels the bottom;
   Now on dry earth he stands;
Now round him throng the Fathers
   To press his gory hands;
And now, with shouts and clapping,
   And noise of weeping loud,
He enters through the River-Gate,
   Borne by the joyous crowd.


### LXV.

They gave him of the corn-land,
   That was of public right,
As much as two strong oxen
   Could plough from morn till night;
And they made a molten image,
   And set it up on high,
And there it stands unto this day
   To witness if I lie.


### LXVI.

It stands in the Comitium,
   Plain for all folk to see;
Horatius in his harness,
   Halting upon one knee:
And underneath is written,
   In letters all of gold,
How valiantly he kept the bridge
   In the brave days of old.

### LXVII.

And still his name sounds stirring
    Unto the men of Rome,
As the trumpet-blast that cries to them
    To charge the Volscian home;
And wives still pray to Juno
    For boys with hearts as bold
As his who kept the bridge so well
    In the brave days of old.

### LXVIII.

And in the nights of winter,
    When the cold north winds blow,
And the long howling of the wolves
    Is heard amidst the snow;
When round the lonely cottage
    Roars loud the tempest's din,
And the good logs of Algidus
    Roar louder yet within;

### LXIX.

When the oldest cask is opened,
    And the largest lamp is lit;
When the chestnuts glow in the embers,
    And the kid turns on the spit;
When young and old in circle
    Around the firebrands close;
When the girls are weaving baskets,
    And the lads are shaping bows;

## LXX.

When the goodman mends his armour,
  And trims his helmet's plume;
When the goodwife's shuttle merrily
  Goes flashing through the loom;
With weeping and with laughter
  Still is the story told,
How well Horatius kept the bridge
  In the brave days of old.

# THE

# BATTLE OF THE LAKE REGILLUS.

# BATTLE OF THE LAKE REGILLUS.

THE following poem is supposed to have been produced about ninety years after the lay of Horatius.
Some persons mentioned in the lay of Horatius make
their appearance again, and some appellations and
epithets used in the lay of Horatius have been
purposely repeated: for, in an age of ballad-poetry,
it scarcely ever fails to happen, that certain phrases
come to be appropriated to certain men and things,
and are regularly applied to those men and things
by every minstrel.   Thus we find, both in the Homeric poems and in Hesiod, βίη Ἡρακληείη, περι-
κλυτος Ἀμφιγυήεις, διάκτορος Ἀργειφόντης, ἑπτάπυλος
Θήβη, Ἑλένης ἕνεκ' ἠυκόμοιο.   Thus, too, in our own
national songs, Douglas is almost always the
doughty Douglas: England is merry England: all
the gold is red; and all the ladies are gay.

The principal distinction between the lay of
Horatius and the lay of the Lake Regillus is that
the former is meant to be purely Roman, while the
latter, though national in its general spirit, has a

slight tincture of Greek learning and of Greek
superstition.   The story of the Tarquins, as it has
come down to us, appears to have been compiled from
the works of several popular poets; and one, at
least, of those poets appears to have visited the
Greek colonies in Italy, if not Greece itself, and to
have had some acquaintance with the works of
Homer and Herodotus.   Many of the most striking
adventures of the house of Tarquin, before Lucretia
makes her appearance, have a Greek character.   The
Tarquins themselves are represented as Corinthian
nobles of the great house of the Bacchiadæ, driven
from their country by the tyranny of that Cypselus,
the tale of whose strange escape Herodotus has
related with incomparable simplicity and liveliness.*
Livy and Dionysius tell us that, when Tarquin the
Proud was asked what was the best mode of go-
verning a conquered city, he replied only by beating
down with his staff all the tallest poppies in his
garden.†   This is exactly what Herodotus, in the
passage to which reference has already been made,
relates of the counsel given to Periander, the son of
Cypselus.   The stratagem by which the town of
Gabii is brought under the power of the Tarquins
is, again, obviously copied from Herodotus.‡   The
embassy of the young Tarquins to the oracle at

* Herodotus, v. 92.   Livy, i. 34.   Dionysius, iii. 46.
† Livy, i. 54.   Dionysius, iv. 50.
‡ Herodotus, iii. 154.   Livy, i. 53.

Delphi is just such a story as would be told by a poet whose head was full of the Greek mythology; and the ambiguous answer returned by Apollo is in the exact style of the prophecies which, according to Herodotus, lured Crœsus to destruction. Then the character of the narrative changes. From the first mention of Lucretia to the retreat of Porsena nothing seems to be borrowed from foreign sources. The villany of Sextus, the suicide of his victim, the revolution, the death of the sons of Brutus, the defence of the bridge, Mucius burning his hand,* Clœlia swimming through Tiber, seem to be all strictly Roman. But when we have done with the Tuscan war, and enter upon the war with the Latines, we are again struck by the Greek air of the story. The Battle of the Lake Regillus is in all respects a Homeric battle, except that the combatants ride astride on their horses, instead of driving chariots. The mass of fighting men is hardly mentioned. The leaders single each other out, and engage hand to hand. The great object of the warriors on both sides is, as in the Iliad, to obtain possession of the spoils and bodies of the slain; and several circumstances are related which forcibly remind us of the great slaughter round the corpses of Sarpedon and Patroclus.

* M. de Pouilly attempted, a hundred and twenty years ago, to prove that the story of Mucius was of Greek origin; but he was signally confuted by the Abbé Sallier. See the *Mémoires de l'Académie des Inscriptions*, vi. 27. 00.

But there is one circumstance which deserves especial notice. Both the war of Troy and the war of Regillus were caused by the licentious passions of young princes, who were therefore peculiarly bound not to be sparing of their own persons in the day of battle. Now the conduct of Sextus at Regillus, as described by Livy, so exactly resembles that of Paris, as described at the beginning of the third book of the Iliad, that it is difficult to believe the resemblance accidental. Paris appears before the Trojan ranks, defying the bravest Greek to encounter him :

> Τρωσὶν μὲν προμάχιζεν ᾿Αλέξανδρος Θεοειδὴς,
> . . . . ᾿Αργείων προκαλίζετο πάντας ἀρίστους,
> ἀντίβιον μαχέσασθαι ἐν αἰνῇ δηϊοτῆτι.

Livy introduces Sextus in a similar manner : 'Ferocem juvenem Tarquinium, ostentantem se in prima exsulum acie.' Menelaus rushes to meet Paris. A Roman noble, eager for vengeance, spurs his horse towards Sextus. Both the guilty princes are instantly terror-stricken :

> Τὸν δ᾿ ὡς οὖν ἐνόησεν ᾿Αλέξανδρος Θεοειδὴς
> ἐν προμάχοισι φανέντα, κατεπλήγη φίλον ἦτορ·
> ἂψ δ᾿ ἑτάρων εἰς ἔθνος ἐχάζετο κῆρ᾿ ἀλεείνων.

'Tarquinius,' says Livy, 'retro in agmen suorum infenso cessit hosti.' If this be a fortuitous coincidence, it is one of the most extraordinary in literature.

In the following poem, therefore, images and incidents have been borrowed, not merely without scruple, but on principle, from the incomparable battle-pieces of Homer.

The popular belief at Rome, from an early period, seems to have been that the event of the great day of Regillus was decided by supernatural agency. Castor and Pollux, it was said, had fought, armed and mounted, at the head of the legions of the commonwealth, and had afterwards carried the news of the victory with incredible speed to the city. The well in the Forum at which they had alighted was pointed out. Near the well rose their ancient temple. A great festival was kept to their honour on the Ides of Quintilis, supposed to be the anniversary of the battle; and on that day sumptuous sacrifices were offered to them at the public charge. One spot on the margin of Lake Regillus was regarded during many ages with superstitious awe. A mark, resembling in shape a horse's hoof, was discernible in the volcanic rock; and this mark was believed to have been made by one of the celestial chargers.

How the legend originated cannot now be ascertained: but we may easily imagine several ways in which it might have originated; nor is it at all necessary to suppose, with Julius Frontinus, that two young men were dressed up by the Dictator to personate the sons of Leda. It is probable that

Livy is correct when he says that the Roman general, in the hour of peril, vowed a temple to Castor.
If so, nothing could be more natural than that the
multitude should ascribe the victory to the favour
of the Twin Gods.   When such was the prevailing
sentiment, any man who chose to declare that, in
the midst of the confusion and slaughter, he had
seen two godlike forms on white horses scattering
the Latines, would find ready credence.   We know,
indeed, that, in modern times, a very similar story
actually found credence among a people much more
civilised than the Romans of the fifth century before
Christ.   A chaplain of Cortes, writing about thirty
years after the conquest of Mexico, in an age of
printing presses, libraries, universities, scholars,
logicians, jurists, and statesmen, had the face to
assert that, in one engagement against the Indians,
Saint James had appeared on a grey horse at the
head of the Castilian adventurers.   Many of those
adventurers were living when this lie was printed.
One of them, honest Bernal Diaz, wrote an account
of the expedition.   He had the evidence of his own
senses against the legend ; but he seems to have
distrusted even the evidence of his own senses.   He
says that he was in the battle, and that he saw a
grey horse with a man on his back, but that the
man was, to his thinking, Francesco de Morla, and
not the ever-blessed apostle Saint James.   'Never-
theless,' Bernal adds, 'it may be that the person

on the grey horse was the glorious apostle Saint
James, and that I, sinner that I am, was unworthy
to see him.' The Romans of the age of Cincinnatus
were probably quite as crédulous as the Spanish
subjects of Charles the Fifth.   It is therefore con-
ceivable that the appearance of Castor and Pollux
may have become an article of faith before the
generation which had fought at Regillus had passed
away.   Nor could anything be more natural than
that the poets of the next age should embellish this
story, and make the celestial horsemen bear the
tidings of victory to Rome.

Many years after the temple of the Twin Gods
had been built in the Forum, an important addition
was made to the ceremonial by which the state annually testified its gratitude for their protection.
Quintus Fabius and Publius Decius were elected
Censors at a momentous crisis.   It had become ab-
solutely necessary that the classification of the
citizens should be revised.   On that classification
depended the distribution of political power.
Party-spirit ran high; and the republic seemed
to be in danger of falling under the dominion
either of a narrow oligarchy or of an ignorant
and headstrong rabble.   Under such circumstances, the most illustrious patrician and the
most illustrious plebeian of the age were intrusted
with the office of arbitrating between the angry
factions; and they performed their arduous task

to the satisfaction of all honest and reasonable
men.

One of their reforms was a remodelling of the
equestrian order; and, having effected this reform,
they determined to give to their work a sanction
derived from religion.  In the chivalrous societies
of modern times, societies which have much more
than may at first sight appear in common with the
equestrian order of Rome, it has been usual to in-
voke the special protection of some Saint, and to
observe his day with peculiar solemnity.  Thus the
Companions of the Garter wear the image of Saint
George depending from their collars, and meet, on
great occasions, in Saint George's Chapel.  Thus,
when Lewis the Fourteenth instituted a new order
of chivalry for the rewarding of military merit, he
commended it to the favour of his own glorified
ancestor and patron, and decreed that all the
members of the fraternity should meet at the royal
palace on the feast of Saint Lewis, should attend
the king to chapel, should hear mass, and should
subsequently hold their great annual assembly.
There is a considerable resemblance between this
rule of the order of Saint Lewis and the rule which
Fabius and Decius made respecting the Roman
knights.  It was ordained that a grand muster and
inspection of the equestrian body should be part
of the ceremonial performed, on the anniversary
of the battle of Regillus, in honour of Castor and

Pollux, the two equestrian Gods.   All the knights, clad in purple and crowned with olive, were to meet at a temple of Mars in the suburbs.   Thence they were to ride in state to the Forum, where the temple of the Twins stood.   This pageant was, during several centuries, considered as one of the most splendid sights of Rome.   In the time of Dionysius the cavalcade sometimes consisted of five thousand horsemen, all persons of fair repute and easy fortune.*

There can be no doubt that the Censors who instituted this august ceremony acted in concert with the Pontiffs to whom, by the constitution of Rome, the superintendence of the public worship belonged; and it is probable that those high religious functionaries were, as usual, fortunate enough to find in their books or traditions some warrant for the innovation.

The following poem is supposed to have been made for this great occasion.   Songs, we know, were chanted at the religious festivals of Rome from an early period; indeed from so early a period, that some of the sacred verses were popularly ascribed to Numa, and were utterly unintelligible in the age of Augustus.   In the Second Punic War

* See Livy, ix. 46.   Val. Max. ii. 2.   Aurel. Vict. De Viris Illustribus, 32.   Dionysius, vi. 13.   Plin. Hist. Nat. xv. 5.   See also the singularly ingenious chapter in Niebuhr's posthumous volume, *Die Censur des Q. Fabius und P. Decius.*

a great feast was held in honour of Juno, and a
song was sung in her praise.  This song was extant when Livy wrote; and, though exceedingly
rugged and uncouth, seemed to him not wholly
destitute of merit.*    A song, as we learn from
Horace,† was part of the established ritual at the
great Secular Jubilee.  It is therefore likely that
the Censors and Pontiffs, when they had resolved to
add a grand procession of knights to the other
solemnities annually performed on the Ides of
Quintilis, would call in the aid of a poet.  Such a
poet would naturally take for his subject the battle
of Regillus, the appearance of the Twin Gods, and
the institution of their festival.  He would find
abundant materials in the ballads of his predeces-
sors; and he would make free use of the scanty
stock of Greek learning which he had himself acquired.  He would probably introduce some wise
and holy Pontiff enjoining the magnificent ceremonial which, after a long interval, had at length
been adopted.  If the poem succeeded, many persons would commit it to memory.  Parts of it
would be sung to the pipe at banquets.  It would
be peculiarly interesting to the great Posthumian
House, which numbered among its many images
that of the Dictator Aulus, the hero of Regillus.
The orator who, in the following generation, pronounced the funeral panegyric over the remains of

* Livy, xxvii. 37.          † Hor. Carmen Seculare.

Lucius Posthumius Megellus, thrice Consul, would borrow largely from the lay; and thus some passages, much disfigured, would probably find their way into the chronicles which were afterwards in the hands of Dionysius and Livy.

Antiquaries differ widely as to the situation of the field of battle. The opinion of those who suppose that the armies met near Cornufelle, between Frascati and the Monte Porzio, is at least plausible, and has been followed in the poem.

As to the details of the battle, it has not been thought desirable to adhere minutely to the accounts which have come down to us. Those accounts, indeed, differ widely from each other, and, in all probability, differ as widely from the ancient poem from which they were originally derived.

It is unnecessary to point out the obvious imitations of the Iliad, which have been purposely introduced.

# THE

# BATTLE OF THE LAKE REGILLUS.

A LAY SUNG AT THE FEAST OF CASTOR AND POLLUX
ON THE IDES OF QUINTILIS,
IN THE YEAR OF THE CITY CCCCLI.

---

## I.

Ho, trumpets, sound a war-note!
  Ho, lictors, clear the way!
The Knights will ride, in all their pride,
  Along the streets to-day.
To-day the doors and windows
  Are hung with garlands all,
From Castor in the Forum,
  To Mars without the wall.
Each Knight is robed in purple,
  With olive each is crowned;
A gallant war-horse under each
  Paws haughtily the ground.
While flows the Yellow River,
  While stands the Sacred Hill,
The proud Ides of Quintilis
  Shall have such honour still.

Gay are the Martian Kalends:
    December's Nones are gay:
But the proud Ides, when the squadron rides,
    Shall be Rome's whitest day.


## II.

Unto the Great Twin Brethren
    We keep this solemn feast.
Swift, swift, the Great Twin Brethren
    Came spurring from the east.
They came o'er wild Parthenius
    Tossing in waves of pine,
O'er Cirrha's dome, o'er Adria's foam,
    O'er purple Apennine,
From where with flutes and dances
    Their ancient mansion rings,
In lordly Lacedæmon,
    The City of two kings,
To where, by Lake Regillus,
    Under the Porcian height,
All in the lands of Tusculum,
    Was fought the glorious fight.


## III.

Now on the place of slaughter
    Are cots and sheepfolds seen,
And rows of vines, and fields of wheat,
    And apple-orchards green;

The swine crush the big acorns
  That fall from Corne's oaks.
Upon the turf by the Fair Fount
  The reaper's pottage smokes.
The fisher baits his angle ;
  The hunter twangs his bow ;
Little they think on those strong limbs
  That moulder deep below.
Little they think how sternly
  That day the trumpets pealed ;
How in the slippery swamp of blood
  Warrior and war-horse reeled ;
How wolves came with fierce gallop,
  And crows on eager wings,
To tear the flesh of captains,
  And peck the eyes of kings ;
How thick the dead lay scattered
  Under the Porcian height ;
How through the gates of Tusculum
  Raved the wild stream of flight ;
And how the Lake Regillus
  Bubbled with crimson foam,
What time the Thirty Cities
  Came forth to war with Rome.


IV.


But, Roman, when thou standest
  Upon that holy ground,
Look thou with heed on the dark rock
  That girds the dark lake round.

F

So shalt thou see a hoof-mark
　　Stamped deep into the flint:
It was no hoof of mortal steed
　　That made so strange a dint:
There to the Great Twin Brethren
　　Vow thou thy vows, and pray
That they, in tempest and in fight,
　　Will keep thy head alway.


v.


Since last the Great Twin Brethren
　　Of mortal eyes were seen,
Have years gone by an hundred
　　And fourscore and thirteen.
That summer a Virginius
　　Was Consul first in place;
The second was stout Aulus,
　　Of the Posthumian race.
The Herald of the Latines
　　From Gabii came in state:
The Herald of the Latines
　　Passed through Rome's Eastern Gate:
The Herald of the Latines
　　Did in our Forum stand;
And there he did his office,
　　A sceptre in his hand.


VI.


‘ Hear, Senators and people
　　Of the good town of Rome,

The Thirty Cities charge you
    To bring the Tarquins home :
And if ye still be stubborn,
    To work the Tarquins wrong,
The Thirty Cities warn you,
    Look that your walls be strong.'


### VII.

Then spake the Consul Aulus,
    He spake a bitter jest :
' Once the jays sent a message
    Unto the eagle's nest :—
Now yield thou up thine eyrie
    Unto the carrion-kite,
Or come forth valiantly, and face
    The jays in deadly fight.—
Forth looked in wrath the eagle ;
    And carrion-kite and jay,
Soon as they saw his beak and claw,
    Fled screaming far away.'


### VIII.

The Herald of the Latines
    Hath hied him back in state :
The Fathers of the City
    Are met in high debate.
Then spake the elder Consul,
    An ancient man and wise :
' Now hearken, Conscript Fathers,
    To that which I advise.

In seasons of great peril
    'Tis good that one bear sway ;
Then choose we a Dictator,
    Whom all men shall obey.
Camerium knows how deeply
    The sword of Aulus bites,
And all our city calls him
    The man of seventy fights.
Then let him be Dictator
    For six months and no more,
And have a Master of the Knights,
    And axes twenty-four.'


IX.


So Aulus was Dictator,
    The man of seventy fights ;
He made Æbutius Elva
    His Master of the Knights.
On the third morn thereafter,
    At dawning of the day,
Did Aulus and Æbutius
    Set forth with their array.
Sempronius Atratinus
    Was left in charge at home
With boys, and with grey-headed men,
    To keep the walls of Rome.
Hard by the Lake Regillus
    Our camp was pitched at night :
Eastward a mile the Latines lay,
    Under the Porcian height.

Far over hill and valley
  Their mighty host was spread;
And with their thousand watch-fires
  The midnight sky was red.


X.


Up rose the golden morning
  Over the Porcian height,
The proud Ides of Quintilis
  Marked evermore with white.
Not without secret trouble
  Our bravest saw the foes;
For girt by threescore thousand spears,
  The thirty standards rose.
From every warlike city
  That boasts the Latian name,
Foredoomed to dogs and vultures,
  That gallant army came;
From Setia's purple vineyards,
  From Norba's ancient wall,
From the white streets of Tusculum,
  The proudest town of all;
From where the Witch's Fortress
  O'erhangs the dark-blue seas;
From the still glassy lake that sleeps
  Beneath Aricia's trees —
Those trees in whose dim shadow
  The ghastly priest doth reign,
The priest who slew the slayer,
  And shall himself be slain;

From the drear banks of Ufens,
  Where flights of marsh-fowl play,
And buffaloes lie wallowing
  Through the hot summer's day ;
From the gigantic watch-towers,
  No work of earthly men,
Whence Cora's sentinels o'erlook
  The never-ending fen ;
From the Laurentian jungle,
  The wild hog's reedy home ;
From the green steeps whence Anio leaps
  In floods of snow-white foam.


                    XI.


Aricia, Cora, Norba,
  Velitræ, with the might
Of Setia and of Tusculum,
  Were marshalled on the right:
The leader was Mamilius,
  Prince of the Latian name ;
Upon his head a helmet
  Of red gold shone like flame :
High on a gallant charger
  Of dark-grey hue he rode ;
Over his gilded armour
  A vest of purple flowed,
Woven in the land of sunrise
  By Syria's dark-browed daughters,
And by the sails of Carthage brought
  Far o'er the southern waters.

XII.

Lavinium and Laurentum
  Had on the left their post,
With all the banners of the marsh,
  And banners of the coast.
Their leader was false Sextus,
  That wrought the deed of shame :
With restless pace and haggard face
  To his last field he came.
Men said he saw strange visions
  Which none beside might see,
And that strange sounds were in his ears
  Which none might hear but he.
A woman fair and stately,
  But pale as are the dead,
Oft through the watches of the night
  Sat spinning by his bed.
And as she plied the distaff,
  In a sweet voice and low,
She sang of great old houses,
  And fights fought long ago.
So spun she, and so sang she,
  Until the east was grey,
Then pointed to her bleeding breast,
  And shrieked, and fled away.


XIII.

But in the centre thickest
  Were ranged the shields of foes,
And from the centre loudest
  The cry of battle rose.

There Tibur marched and Pedum
   Beneath proud Tarquin's rule,
And Ferentinum of the rock,
   And Gabii of the pool.
There rode the Volscian succours:
   There, in a dark stern ring,
The Roman exiles gathered close
   Around the ancient king.
Though white as Mount Soracte,
   When winter nights are long,
His beard flowed down o'er mail and belt,
   His heart and hand were strong:
Under his hoary eyebrows
   Still flashed forth quenchless rage,
And, if the lance shook in his gripe,
   'Twas more with hate than age.
Close at his side was Titus
   On an Apulian steed,
Titus, the youngest Tarquin,
   Too good for such a breed.


XIV.

Now on each side the leaders
   Give signal for the charge;
And on each side the footmen
   Strode on with lance and targe;
And on each side the horsemen
   Struck their spurs deep in gore;
And front to front the armies
   Met with a mighty roar:

And under that great battle
  The earth with blood was red;
And, like the Pomptine fog at morn,
  The dust hung overhead;
And louder still and louder
  Rose from the darkened field
The braying of the war-horns,
  The clang of sword and shield,
The rush of squadrons sweeping
  Like whirlwinds o'er the plain,
The shouting of the slayers,
  And screeching of the slain.


                XV.

False Sextus rode out foremost:
  His look was high and bold;
His corslet was of bison's hide,
  Plated with steel and gold.
As glares the famished eagle
  From the Digentian rock
On a choice lamb that bounds alone
  Before Bandusia's flock,
Herminius glared on Sextus,
  And came with eagle speed,
Herminius on black Auster,
  Brave champion on brave steed;
In his right hand the broadsword
  That kept the bridge so well,
And on his helm the crown he won
  When proud Fidenæ fell.

Woe to the maid whose lover
   Shall cross his path to-day!
False Sextus saw, and trembled,
   And turned, and fled away.
As turns, as flies, the woodman
   In the Calabrian brake,
When through the reeds gleams the round eye
   Of that fell speckled snake;
So turned, so fled, false Sextus,
   And hid him in the rear,
Behind the dark Lavinian ranks,
   Bristling with crest and spear.


### XVI.

But far to north Æbutius,
   The Master of the Knights,
Gave Tubero of Norba
   To feed the Porcian kites.
Next under those red horse-hoofs
   Flaccus of Setia lay;
Better had he been pruning
   Among his elms that day.
Mamilius saw the slaughter,
   And tossed his golden crest,
And towards the Master of the Knights
   Through the thick battle pressed.
Æbutius smote Mamilius
   So fiercely on the shield
That the great lord of Tusculum
   Well nigh rolled on the field.

Mamilius smote Æbutius,
  With a good aim and true,
Just where the neck and shoulder join,
  And pierced him through and through ;
And brave Æbutius Elva
  Fell swooning to the ground :
But a thick wall of bucklers
  Encompassed him around.
His clients from the battle
  Bare him some little space,
And filled a helm from the dark lake,
  And bathed his brow and face ;
And when at last he opened
  His swimming eyes to light,
Men say, the earliest word he spake
  Was, ' Friends, how goes the fight ? '


## XVII.

But meanwhile in the centre
  Great deeds of arms were wrought;
There Aulus the Dictator
  And there Valerius fought.
Aulus with his good broadsword
  A bloody passage cleared
To where, amidst the thickest foes,
  He saw the long white beard.
Flat lighted that good broadsword
  Upon proud Tarquin's head.
He dropped the lance : he dropped the reins :
  He fell as fall the dead.

Down Aulus springs to slay him,
  With eyes like coals of fire;
But faster Titus hath sprung down,
  And hath bestrode his sire.
Latian captains, Roman knights,
  Fast down to earth they spring,
And hand to hand they fight on foot
  Around the ancient king.
First Titus gave tall Cæso
  A death wound in the face;
Tall Cæso was the bravest man
  Of the brave Fabian race:
Aulus slew Rex of Gabii,
  The priest of Juno's shrine:
Valerius smote down Julius,
  Of Rome's great Julian line;
Julius, who left his mansion
  High on the Velian hill,
And through all turns of weal and woe
  Followed proud Tarquin still.
Now right across proud Tarquin
  A corpse was Julius laid;
And Titus groaned with rage and grief,
  And at Valerius made.
Valerius struck at Titus,
  And lopped off half his crest;
But Titus stabbed Valerius
  A span deep in the breast.
Like a mast snapped by the tempest,
  Valerius reeled and fell.
Ah! woe is me for the good house
  That loves the people well!

Then shouted loud the Latines;
　And with one rush they bore
The struggling Romans backward
　Three lances' length and more:
And up they took proud Tarquin,
　And laid him on a shield,
And four strong yeomen bare him,
　Still senseless, from the field.


XVIII.

But fiercer grew the fighting
　Around Valerius dead;
For Titus dragged him by the foot,
　And Aulus by the head.
'On, Latines, on!' quoth Titus,
　'See how the rebels fly!'
'Romans, stand firm!' quoth Aulus,
　'And win this fight or die!
They must not give Valerius
　To raven and to kite;
For aye Valerius loathed the wrong,
　And aye upheld the right:
And for your wives and babies
　In the front rank he fell.
Now play the men for the good house
　That loves the people well!'


XIX.

Then tenfold round the body
　The roar of battle rose,

Like the roar of a burning forest,
  When a strong north wind blows.
Now backward, and now forward,
  Rocked furiously the fray,
Till none could see Valerius,
  And none wist where he lay.
For shivered arms and ensigns
  Were heaped there in a mound,
And corpses stiff, and dying men
  That writhed and gnawed the ground;
And wounded horses kicking,
  And snorting purple foam:
Right well did such a couch befit
  A Consular of Rome.


### XX.

But north looked the Dictator;
  North looked he long and hard;
And spake to Caius Cossus,
  The Captain of his Guard;
'Caius, of all the Romans
  Thou hast the keenest sight;
Say, what through yonder storm of dust
  Comes from the Latian right?'


### XXI.

Then answered Caius Cossus:
  'I see an evil sight;
The banner of proud Tusculum
  Comes from the Latian right;

I see the plumed horsemen;
    And far before the rest
I see the dark-grey charger,
    I see the purple vest ;
I see the golden helmet
    That shines far off like flame ;
So ever rides Mamilius,
    Prince of the Latian name.'


### XXII.

' Now hearken, Caius Cossus:
    Spring on thy horse's back ;
Ride as the wolves of Apennino
    Were all upon thy track ;
Haste to our southward battle:
    And never draw thy rein
Until thou find Herminius,
    And bid him come amain.'


### XXIII.

So Aulus spake, and turned him
    Again to that fierce strife ;
And Caius Cossus mounted,
    And rode for death and life.
Loud clanged beneath his horse-hoofs
    The helmets of the dead,
And many a curdling pool of blood
    Splashed him from heel to head.
So came he far to southward,
    Where fought the Roman host,

Against the banners of the marsh
  And banners of the coast.
Like corn before the sickle
  The stout Lavinians fell,
Beneath the edge of the true sword
  That kept the bridge so well.


### XXIV.

'Herminius! Aulus greets thee;
  He bids thee come with speed,
To help our central battle;
  For sore is there our need.
There wars the youngest Tarquin,
  And there the Crest of Flame,
The Tusculan Mamilius,
  Prince of the Latian name.
Valerius hath fallen fighting
  In front of our array:
And Aulus of the seventy fields
  Alone upholds the day.'


### XXV.

Herminius beat his bosom:
  But never a word he spake.
He clapped his hand on Auster's mane:
  He gave the reins a shake,
Away, away went Auster,
  Like an arrow from the bow:
Black Auster was the fleetest steed
  From Aufidus to Po.

### XXVI.

Right glad were all the Romans
    Who, in that hour of dread,
Against great odds bare up the war
    Around Valerius dead,
When from the south the cheering
    Rose with a mighty swell;
'Herminius comes, Herminius,
    Who kept the bridge so well!'

### XXVII.

Mamilius spied Herminius,
    And dashed across the way.
'Herminius! I have sought thee
    Through many a bloody day.
One of us two, Herminius,
    Shall never more go home.
I will lay on for Tusculum,
    And lay thou on for Rome!'

### XXVIII.

All round them paused the battle,
    While met in mortal fray
The Roman and the Tusculan,
    The horses black and grey.
Herminius smote Mamilius
    Through breast-plate and through breast;
And fast flowed out the purple blood
    Over the purple vest.
Mamilius smote Herminius
    Through head-piece and through head;

And side by side those chiefs of pride
  Together fell down dead.
Down fell they dead together
  In a great lake of gore;
And still stood all who saw them fall
  While men might count a score.


### XXIX.

Fast, fast, with heels wild spurning,
  The dark-grey charger fled:
He burst through ranks of fighting men;
  He sprang o'er heaps of dead,
His bridle far out-streaming,
  His flanks all blood and foam,
He sought the southern mountains,
  The mountains of his home.
The pass was steep and rugged,
  The wolves they howled and whined;
But he ran like a whirlwind up the pass,
  And he left the wolves behind.
Through many a startled hamlet
  Thundered his flying feet;
He rushed through the gate of Tusculum,
  He rushed up the long white street;
He rushed by tower and temple,
  And paused not from his race
Till he stood before his master's door
  In the stately market-place.
And straightway round him gathered
  A pale and trembling crowd,

And when they knew him, cries of rage
  Brake forth, and wailing loud :
And women rent their tresses
  For their great prince's fall ;
And old men girt on their old swords,
  And went to man the wall.


### XXX.

But, like a graven image,
  Black Auster kept his place,
And ever wistfully he looked
  Into his master's face.
The raven-mane that daily,
  With pats and fond caresses,
The young Herminia washed and combed,
  And twined in even tresses,
And decked with coloured ribands
  From her own gay attire,
Hung sadly o'er her father's corpse
  In carnage and in mire.
Forth with a shout sprang Titus,
  And seized black Auster's rein.
Then Aulus sware a fearful oath,
  And ran at him amain.
'The furies of thy brother
  With me and mine abide,
If one of your accursed house
  Upon black Auster ride ! '
As on an Alpine watch-tower
  From heaven comes down the flame,

Full on the neck of Titus
  The blade of Aulus came:
And out the red blood spouted,
  In a wide arch and tall,
As spouts a fountain in the court
  Of some rich Capuan's hall.
The knees of all the Latines
  Were loosened with dismay
When dead, on dead Herminius,
  The bravest Tarquin lay.


XXXI.

And Aulus the Dictator
  Stroked Auster's raven mane,
With heed he looked unto the girths,
  With heed unto the rein.
'Now bear me well, black Auster,
  'Into yon thick array;
And thou and I will have revenge
  For thy good lord this day.'


XXXII.

So spake he; and was buckling
  Tighter black Auster's band,
When he was aware of a princely pair
  That rode at his right hand.
So like they were, no mortal
  Might one from other know:
White as snow their armour was:
  Their steeds were white as snow.

Never on earthly anvil
　　Did such rare armour gleam;
And never did such gallant steeds
　　Drink of an earthly stream.


### XXXIII.

And all who saw them trembled,
　　And pale grew every cheek;
And Aulus the Dictator
　　Scarce gathered voice to speak.
'Say by what name men call you?
　　What city is your home?
And wherefore ride ye in such guise
　　Before the ranks of Rome?'


### XXXIV.

'By many names men call us;
　　In many lands we dwell:
Well Samothracia knows us;
　　Cyrene knows us well.
Our house in gay Tarentum
　　Is hung each morn with flowers:
High o'er the masts of Syracuse
　　Our marble portal towers;
But by the proud Eurotas
　　Is our dear native home;
And for the right we come to fight
　　Before the ranks of Rome.'

### XXXV.

So answered those strange horsemen,
  And each couched low his spear ;
And forthwith all the ranks of Rome
  Were bold, and of good cheer :
And on the thirty armies
  Came wonder and affright,
And Ardea wavered on the left,
  And Cora on the right.
' Rome to the charge ! ' cried Aulus ;
  ' The foe begins to yield !
Charge for the hearth of Vesta !
  Charge for the Golden Shield !
Let no man stop to plunder,
  But slay, and slay, and slay ;
The Gods who live for ever
  Are on our side to-day.'

### XXXVI.

Then the fierce trumpet-flourish
  From earth to heaven arose,
The kites know well the long stern swell
  That bids the Romans close.
Then the good sword of Aulus
  Was lifted up to slay :
Then, like a crag down Apennine,
  Rushed Auster through the fray.
But under those strange horsemen
  Still thicker lay the slain ;
And after those strange horses
  Black Auster toiled in vain.

Behind them Rome's long battle
  Came rolling on the foe,
Ensigns dancing wild above,
  Blades all in line below.
So comes the Po in flood-time
  Upon the Celtic plain :
So comes the squall, blacker than night,
  Upon the Adrian main.
Now, by our Sire Quirinus,
  It was a goodly sight
To see the thirty standards
  Swept down the tide of flight.
So flies the spray of Adria
  When the black squall doth blow,
So corn-sheaves in the flood-time
  Spin down the whirling Po.
False Sextus to the mountains
  Turned first his horse's head ;
And fast fled Ferentinum,
  And fast Lanuvium fled.
The horsemen of Nomentum
  Spurred hard out of the fray ;
The footmen of Velitræ
  Threw shield and spear away.
And underfoot was trampled,
  Amidst the mud and gore,
The banner of proud Tusculum,
  That never stooped before :
And down went Flavius Faustus,
  Who led his stately ranks
From where the apple blossoms wave
  On Anio's echoing banks,

And Tullus of Arpinum,
    Chief of the Volscian aids,
And Metius with the long fair curls,
    The love of Anxur's maids,
And the white head of Vulso,
    The great Arician seer,
And Nepos of Laurentum,
    The hunter of the deer;
And in the back false Sextus
    Felt the good Roman steel,
And wriggling in the dust he died,
    Like a worm beneath the wheel :
And fliers and pursuers
    Were mingled in a mass ;
And far away the battle
    Went roaring through the pass.


### XXXVII.

Sempronius Atratinus
    Sate in the Eastern Gate,
Beside him were three Fathers,
    Each in his chair of state ;
Fabius, whose nine stout grandsons
    That day were in the field,
And Manlius, eldest of the Twelve
    Who kept the Golden Shield ;
And Sergius, the High Pontiff,
    For wisdom far renowned ;
In all Etruria's colleges
    Was no such Pontiff found.

And all around the portal,
  And high above the wall,
Stood a great throng of people,
  But sad and silent all ;
Young lads, and stooping elders
  That might not bear the mail,
·Matrons with lips that quivered,
  And maids with faces pale.
Since the first gleam of daylight,
  Sempronius had not ceased
To listen for the rushing
  Of horse-hoofs from the east.
The mist of eve was rising,
  The sun was hastening down,
When he was aware of a princely pair
  Fast pricking towards the town.
So like they were, man never
  Saw twins so like before ;
Red with gore their armour was,
  Their steeds were red with gore.


XXXVIII.

'Hail to the great Asylum !
  Hail to the hill-tops seven !
Hail to the fire that burns for aye,
  And the shield that fell from heaven !
This day, by Lake Regillus,
  Under the Porcian height,
All in the lands of Tusculum
  Was fought a glorious fight,

To-morrow your Dictator
  Shall bring in triumph home
The spoils of thirty cities
  To deck the shrines of Rome!'


### XXXIX.

Then burst from that great concourse
  A shout that shook the towers,
And some ran north, and some ran south,
  Crying, 'The day is ours!'
But on rode these strange horsemen,
  With slow and lordly pace;
And none who saw their bearing
  Durst ask their name or race.
On rode they to the Forum,
  While laurel-boughs and flowers,
From house-tops and from windows,
  Fell on their crests in showers.
When they drew nigh to Vesta,
  They vaulted down amain,
And washed their horses in the well
  That springs by Vesta's fane.
And straight again they mounted,
  And rode to Vesta's door;
Then, like a blast, away they passed,
  And no man saw them more.


### XL.

And all the people trembled,
  And pale grew every cheek;

And Sergius the High Pontiff
  Alone found voice to speak :
' The gods who live for ever
  Have fought for Rome to-day !
These be the Great Twin Brethren
  To whom the Dorians pray.
Back comes the Chief in triumph,
  Who, in the hour of fight,
Hath seen the Great Twin Brethren
  In harness on his right.
Safe comes the ship to haven,
  Through billows and through gales,
If once the Great Twin Brethren
  Sit shining on the sails.
Wherefore they washed their horses
  In Vesta's holy well,
Wherefore they rode to Vesta's door,
  I know, but may not tell.
Here, hard by Vesta's Temple,
  Build we a stately dome
Unto the Great Twin Brethren
  Who fought so well for Rome.
And when the months returning
  Bring back this day of fight,
The proud Ides of Quintilis,
  Marked evermore with white,
Unto the Great Twin Brethren
  Let all the people throng,
With chaplets and with offerings,
  With music and with song ;
And let the doors and windows
  Be hung with garlands all,

And let the Knights be summoned
   ' To Mars without the wall :
Thence let them ride in purple
   With joyous trumpet-sound,
Each mounted on his war-horse,
   And each with olive crowned ;
And pass in solemn order
   Before the sacred dome,
Where dwell the Great Twin Brethren
   Who fought so well for Rome ! '

# VIRGINIA.

# VIRGINIA.

A COLLECTION consisting exclusively of war-songs would give an imperfect, or rather an erroneous, notion of the spirit of the old Latin ballads. The Patricians, during more than a century after the expulsion of the Kings, held all the high military commands. A Plebeian, even though, like Lucius Siccius, he were distinguished by his valour and knowledge of war, could serve only in subordinate posts. A minstrel, therefore, who wished to celebrate the early triumphs of his country, could hardly take any but Patricians for his heroes. The warriors who are mentioned in the two preceding lays, Horatius, Lartius, Herminius, Aulus Posthumius, Æbutius Elva, Sempronius Atratinus, Valerius Poplicola, were all members of the dominant order; and a poet who was singing their praises, whatever his own political opinions might be, would naturally abstain from insulting the class to which they belonged, and from reflecting on the system which had placed such men at the head of the legions of the Commonwealth.

But there was a class of compositions in which

the great families were by no means so courteously treated. No parts of early Roman history are richer with poetical colouring than those which relate to the long contest between the privileged houses and the commonalty. The population of Rome was, from a very early period, divided into hereditary castes, which, indeed, readily united to repel foreign enemies, but which regarded each other, during many years, with bitter animosity. Between those castes there was a barrier hardly less strong than that which, at Venice, parted the members of the Great Council from their countrymen. In some respects, indeed, the line which separated an Icilius or a Duilius from a Posthumius or a Fabius was even more deeply marked than that which separated the rower of a gondola from a Contarini or a Morosini. At Venice the distinction was merely civil. At Rome it was both civil and religious. Among the grievances under which the Plebeians suffered, three were felt as peculiarly severe. They were excluded from the highest magistracies; they were excluded from all share in the public lands; and they were ground down to the dust by partial and barbarous legislation touching pecuniary contracts. The ruling class in Rome was a monied class; and it made and administered the laws with a view solely to its own interest. Thus the relation between lender and borrower was mixed up with the relation between sovereign

and subject. The great men held a large portion
of the community in dependence by means of advances at enormous usury. The law of debt, framed
by creditors, and for the protection of creditors,
was the most horrible that has ever been known
among men. The liberty, and even the life, of the
insolvent were at the mercy of the Patrician money-
lenders. Children often became slaves in consequence of the misfortunes of their parents. The
debtor was imprisoned, not in a public gaol under
the care of impartial public functionaries, but in
a private workhouse belonging to the creditor.
Frightful stories were told respecting these dun-
geons. It was said that torture and brutal violation
were common; that ,tight stocks, heavy chains,
scanty measures of food, were used to punish
wretches guilty of nothing but poverty; and that
brave soldiers, whose breasts were covered with
honourable scars, were often marked still more
deeply on the back by the scourges of high-born
usurers.

The Plebeians were, however, not wholly without
constitutional rights. From an early period they
had been admitted to some share of political power.
They were enrolled each in his century, and were
allowed a share, considerable though not propor-
tioned to their numerical strength, in the disposal
of those high dignities from which they were themselves excluded. Thus their position bore some

H

resemblance to that of the Irish Catholics during
the interval between the year 1792 and the year
1829.   The Plebeians had also the privilege of annually appointing officers, named Tribunes, who had
no active share in the government of the Commonwealth, but who, by degrees, acquired a power for-
midable even to the ablest and most resolute Consuls
and Dictators.   The person of the Tribune was in-
violable; and, though he could directly effect little,
he could obstruct everything.

During more than a century after the institution
of the Tribuneship, the Commons struggled man-
fully for the removal of the grievances under which
they laboured; and, in spite of many checks and
reverses, succeeded in wringing concession after
concession from the stubborn aristocracy.  At length
in the year of the city 378, both parties mustered
their whole strength for their last and most despe-
rate conflict.   The popular and active Tribune,
Caius Licinius, proposed the three memorable laws
which are called by his name, and which were intended to redress the three great evils of which
the Plebeians complained.  He was supported, with
eminent ability and firmness, by his colleague,
Lucius Sextius.  The struggle appears to have
been the fiercest that ever in any community
terminated without an appeal to arms.   If
such a contest had raged in any Greek city, the
streets would have run with blood.   But, even in

the paroxysms of faction, the Roman retained his
gravity, his respect for law, and his tenderness for
the lives of his fellow-citizens. Year after year
Licinius and Sextius were re-elected Tribunes.
Year after year, if the narrative which has come
down to us is to be trusted, they continued to
exert, to the full extent, their power of stopping
the whole machine of government. No curule
magistrates could be chosen; no military muster
could be held. We know too little of the state of
Rome in those days to be able to conjecture how,
during that long anarchy, the peace was kept, and
ordinary justice administered between man and
man. The animosity of both parties rose to the
greatest height. The excitement, we may well
suppose, would have been peculiarly intense at the
annual election of Tribunes. On such occasions
there can be little doubt that the great families
did all that could be done, by threats and caresses,
to break the union of the Plebeians. That union,
however, proved indissoluble. At length the good
cause triumphed. The Licinian laws were carried.
Lucius Sextius was the first Plebeian Consul,
Caius Licinius the third.

The results of this great change were singularly
happy and glorious. Two centuries of prosperity,
harmony, and victory followed the reconciliation
of the orders. Men who remembered Rome en-
gaged in waging petty wars almost within sight of

the Capitol lived to see her the mistress of Italy.
While the disabilities of the Plebeians continued,
she was scarcely able to maintain her ground
against the Volscians and Hernicans.    When
those disabilities were removed, she rapidly became
more than a match for Carthage and Macedon.

During the great Licinian contest the Plebeian
poets were, doubtless, not silent.    Even in modern
times songs have been by no means without influence on public affairs ; and we may therefore infer
that, in a society where printing was unknown,
and where books were rare, a pathetic or humo-
rous party-ballad must have produced effects such
as we can but faintly conceive.    It is certain that
satirical poems were common at Rome from a very
early period.    The rustics, who lived at a distance
from the seat of government, and took little part
in the strife of factions, gave vent to their petty
local animosities in coarse Fescennine verse.    The
lampoons of the city were doubtless of a higher
order ; and their sting was early felt by the
nobility.    For in the Twelve Tables, long before
the time of the Licinian laws, a severe punishment
was denounced against the citizen who should
compose or recite verses reflecting on another.*

* Cicero justly infers from this law that there had been early
Latin poets whose works had been lost before his time.
'Quamquam id quidem etiam xii tabulæ declarant, condi jam
tum solitum esse carmen, quod ne liceret fieri ad alterius in-
juriam lege sanxerunt.'—*Tusc.* iv. 2.

Satire is, indeed, the only sort of composition in which the Latin poets, whose works have come down to us, were not mere imitators of foreign models; and it is therefore the only sort of composition in which they have never been rivalled. It was not, like their tragedy, their comedy, their epic and lyric poetry, a hothouse plant which, in return for assiduous and skilful culture, gave only scanty and sickly fruits. It was hardy and full of sap; and in all the various juices which it yielded might be distinguished the flavour of the Ausonian soil. 'Satire,' says Quinctilian, with just pride, 'is all our own.' Satire sprang, in truth, naturally from the constitution of the Roman government and from the spirit of the Roman people; and, though at length subjected to metrical rules derived from Greece, retained to the last an essentially Roman character. Lucilius was the earliest satirist whose works were held in esteem under the Cæsars. But many years before Lucilius was born, Nævius had been flung into a dungeon, and guarded there with circumstances of unusual rigour, on account of the bitter lines in which he had attacked the great Cæcilian family.* The genius and spirit of the Roman satirist survived the liberty of their country, and were not extinguished by the cruel despotism of the Julian and

---

* Plautus, Miles Gloriosus. Aulus Gellius, lii. 3.

Flavian Emperors. The great poet who told the
story of Domitian's turbot, was the legitimate
successor of those forgotten minstrels whose songs
animated the factions of the infant Republic.

These minstrels, as Niebuhr has remarked,
appear to have generally taken the popular side.
We can hardly be mistaken in supposing that, at
the great crisis of the civil conflict, they employed
themselves in versifying all the most powerful and
virulent speeches of the Tribunes, and in heaping
abuse on the leaders of the aristocracy. Every
personal defect, every domestic scandal, every
tradition dishonourable to a noble house, would be
sought out, brought into notice, and exaggerated.
The illustrious head of the aristocratical party,
Marcus Furius Camillus, might perhaps be, in
some measure, protected by his venerable age and
by the memory of his great services to the State.
But Appius Claudius Crassus enjoyed no such
immunity. He was descended from a long line
of ancestors distinguished by their haughty de-
meanour, and by the inflexibility with which they
had withstood all the demands of the Plebeian
order. While the political conduct and the deport-
ment of the Claudian nobles drew upon them the
fiercest public hatred, they were accused of wanting, if any credit is due to the early history of
Rome, a class of qualities which, in the military
Commonwealth, is sufficient to cover a multitude

of offences. The chiefs of the family appear to have been eloquent, versed in civil business, and learned after the fashion of their age; but in war they were not distinguished by skill or valour. Some of them, as if conscious where their weakness lay, had, when filling the highest magistracies, taken internal administration as their department of public business, and left the military command to their colleagues.* One of them had been intrusted with an army, and had failed ignominiously.† None of them had been honoured with a triumph. None of them had achieved any martial exploit, such as those by which Lucius Quinctius Cincinnatus, Titus Quinctius Capitolinus, Aulus Cornelius Cossus, and, above all, the great Camillus, had extorted the reluctant esteem of the multitude. During the Licinian conflict, Appius Claudius Crassus signalised himself by the ability and severity with which he harangued against the two great agitators. He would naturally, therefore, be the favourite mark of the Plebeian satirists; nor would they have been at a loss to find a point on which he was open to attack.

His grandfather, called, like himself, Appius Claudius, had left a name as much detested as that of Sextus Tarquinius. This elder Appius had been Consul more than seventy years before

* In the years of the city 260, 304, and 330.
† In the year of the city 282.

the introduction of the Licinian laws.  By availing
himself of a singular crisis in public feeling, he
had obtained the consent of the Commons to the
abolition of the Tribuneship, and had been the
chief of that Council of Ten to which the whole
direction of the State had been committed.  In a
few months his administration had become univer-
sally odious.  It had been swept away by an
irresistible outbreak of popular fury; and its
memory was still held in abhorrence by the whole
city.  The immediate cause of the downfall of
this execrable government was said to have been
an attempt made by Appius Claudius upon the
chastity of a beautiful young girl of humble birth.
The story ran that the Decemvir, unable to succeed
by bribes and solicitations, resorted to an out-
rageous act of tyranny.  A vile dependent of the
Claudian house laid claim to the damsel as his
slave.  The cause was brought before the tribunal
of Appius.  The wicked magistrate, in defiance of
the clearest proofs, gave judgment for the claimant.
But the girl's father, a brave soldier, saved her
from servitude and dishonour by stabbing her
to the heart in the sight of the whole Forum.
That blow was the signal for a general explosion.
Camp and city rose at once; the Ten were pulled
down; the Tribuneship was re-established; and
Appius escaped the hands of the executioner only
by a voluntary death.

It can hardly be doubted that a story so admirably adapted to the purposes both of the poet and of the demagogue would be eagerly seized upon by minstrels burning with hatred against the Patrician order, against the Claudian house, and especially against the grandson and namesake of the infamous Decemvir.

In order that the reader may judge fairly of these fragments of the lay of Virginia, he must imagine himself a Plebeian who has just voted for the re-election of Sextius and Licinius. All the power of the Patricians has been exerted to throw out the two great champions of the Commons. Every Posthumius, Æmilius, and Cornelius has used his influence to the utmost. Debtors have been let out of the workhouses on condition of voting against the men of the people : clients have been posted to hiss and interrupt the favourite candidates : Appius Claudius Crassus has spoken with more than his usual eloquence and asperity : all has been in vain ; Licinius and Sextius have a fifth time carried all the tribes: work is suspended : the booths are closed : the Plebeians bear on their shoulders the two champions of liberty through the Forum. Just at this moment it is announced that a popular poet, a zealous adherent of the Tribunes, has made a new song which will cut the Claudian nobles to the heart. The crowd gathers

round him, and calls on him to recite it.   He
takes his stand on the spot where, according to
tradition, Virginia, more than seventy years ago,
was seized by the pandar of Appius, and he begins
his story.

# VIRGINIA.

FRAGMENTS OF A LAY SUNG IN THE FORUM ON THE DAY WHEREON LUCIUS SEXTIUS SEXTINUS LATERANUS AND CAIUS LICINIUS CALVUS STOLO WERE ELECTED TRIBUNES OF THE COMMONS THE FIFTH TIME, IN THE YEAR OF THE CITY CCCLXXXII.

————

YE good men of the Commons, with loving hearts and true,
Who stand by the bold Tribunes that still have stood by you,
Come, make a circle round me, and mark my tale with care,
A tale of what Rome once hath borne, of what Rome yet may bear.
This is no Grecian fable, of fountains running wine,
Of maids with snaky tresses, or sailors turned to swine.
Here, in this very Forum, under the noonday sun,
In sight of all the people, the bloody deed was done.
Old men still creep among us who saw that fearful day,
Just seventy years and seven ago, when the wicked Ten bare sway.

Of all the wicked Ten still the names are held accursed,
And of all the wicked Ten Appius Claudius was the worst.
He stalked along the Forum like King Tarquin in his pride:
Twelve axes waited on him, six marching on a side;
The townsmen shrank to right and left, and eyed askance with fear
His lowering brow, his curling mouth, which always seemed to
    sneer:
That brow of hate, that mouth of scorn, marks all the kindred still;
For never was there Claudius yet but wished the Commons ill:

Nor lacks he fit attendance; for close behind his heels,
With outstretched chin and crouching pace, the client Marcus
    steals,
His loins girt up to run with speed, be the errand what it may,
And the smile flickering on his check, for aught his lord may say.
Such varlets pimp and jest for hire among the lying Greeks :
Such varlets still are paid to hoot when brave Licinius speaks.
Where'er ye shed the honey, the buzzing flies will crowd ;
Where'er ye fling the carrion, the raven's croak is loud ;
Where'er down Tiber garbage floats, the greedy pike ye see ;
And wheresoe'er such lord is found, such client still will be.

   Just then, as through one cloudless chink in a black stormy sky,
Shines out the dewy morning-star, a fair young girl came by.
With her small tablets in her hand, and her satchel on her arm,
Home she went bounding from the school, nor dreamed of shame
    or harm ;
And past those dreaded axes she innocently ran,
With bright, frank brow that had not learned to blush at gaze of
    man;
And up the Sacred Street she turned, and, as she danced along,
She warbled gaily to herself lines of the good old song,
How for a sport the princes came spurring from the camp,
And found Lucrece, combing the fleece, under the midnight lamp.
The maiden sang as sings the lark, when up he darts his flight,
From his nest in the green April corn, to meet the morning light ;
And Appius heard her sweet young voice, and saw her sweet
    young face,
And loved her with the accursed love of his accursed race,
And all along the Forum, and up the Sacred Street,
His vulture eye pursued the trip of those small glancing feet.
    *      *      *      *      *      *      *

Over the Alban mountains the light of morning broke;
From all the roofs of the Seven Hills curled the thin wreaths of
    smoke:
The city-gates were opened; the Forum all alive,
With buyers and with sellers was humming like a hive:
Blithely on brass and timber the craftsman's stroke was ringing,
And blithely o'er her panniers the market-girl was singing,
And blithely young Virginia came smiling from her home:
Ah! woe for young Virginia, the sweetest maid in Rome!
With her small tablets in her hand, and her satchel on her arm,
Forth she went bounding to the school, nor dreamed of shame
    or harm.
She crossed the Forum shining with stalls in alleys gay,
And just had reached the very spot whereon I stand this day,
When up the varlet Marcus came; not such as when erewhile
He crouched behind his patron's heels with the true client smile:
He came with lowering forehead, swollen features, and clenched
    fist,
And strode across Virginia's path, and caught her by the wrist.
Hard strove the frighted maiden, and screamed with look aghast;
And at her scream from right and left the folk came running fast;
The money-changer Crispus, with his thin silver hairs,
And Hanno from the stately booth glittering with Punic wares,
And the strong smith Muræna, grasping a half-forged brand,
And Volero the flesher, his cleaver in his hand.
All came in wrath and wonder; for all knew that fair child;
And, as she passed them twice a day, all kissed their hands and
    smiled;
And the strong smith Muræna gave Marcus such a blow,
The caitiff reeled three paces back, and let the maiden go.
Yet glared he fiercely round him, and growled in harsh, fell tone,
' She's mine, and I will have her: I seek but for mine own:

She is my slave, born in my house, and stolen away and sold,
The year of the sore sickness, ere she was twelve hours old.
'Twas in the sad September, the month of wail and fright,
Two augurs were borne forth that morn; the Consul died ere
    night.
I wait on Appius Claudius, I waited on his sire :
Let him who works the client wrong beware the patron's ire ! '

So spake the varlet Marcus ; and dread and silence came
On all the people at the sound of the great Claudian name.
For then there was no Tribune to speak the word of might,
Which makes the rich man tremble, and guards the poor man's
    right.
There was no brave Licinius, no honest Sextius then ;
But all the city, in great fear, obeyed the wicked Ten.
Yet ere the varlet Marcus again might seize the maid,
Who clung tight to Muræna's skirt, and sobbed, and shrieked for
    aid,
Forth through the throng of gazers the young Icilius pressed,
And stamped his foot, and rent his gown, and smote upon his breast,
And sprang upon that column, by many a minstrel sung,
Whereon three mouldering helmets, three rusting swords, are
    hung.
And beckoned to the people, and in bold voice and clear
Poured thick and fast the burning words which tyrants quake to
    hear.

' Now, by your children's cradles, now by your fathers' graves,
Be men to-day, Quirites, or be for ever slaves !
For this did Servius give us laws ?   For this did Lucrece bleed ?
For this was the great vengeance wrought on Tarquin's evil seed ?
For this did those false sons make red the axes of their sire ?
For this did Scævola's right hand hiss in the Tuscan fire ?

Shall the vile fox-earth awe the race that stormed the lion's den ?
Shall we, who could not brook one lord, crouch to the wicked Ten ?
Oh for that ancient spirit which curbed the Senate's will!
Oh for the tents which in old time whitened the Sacred Hill!
In those brave days our fathers stood firmly side by side ;
They faced the Marcian fury ; they tamed the Fabian pride :
They drove the fiercest Quinctius an outcast forth from Rome ;
They sent the haughtiest Claudius with shivered fasces home.
But what their care bequeathed us our madness flung away :
All the ripe fruit of threescore years was blighted in a day.
Exult, ye proud Patricians! The hard-fought fight is o'er.
We strove for honours—'twas in vain : for freedom—'tis no more.
No crier to the polling summons the eager throng ;
No tribune breathes the word of might that guards the weak
        from wrong.
Our very hearts, that were so high, sink down beneath your will.
Riches, and lands, and power, and state—ye have them :—keep
        them still.
Still keep the holy fillets ; still keep the purple gown,
The axes, and the curule chair, the car, and laurel crown :
Still press us for your cohorts, and, when the fight is done,
Still fill your garners from the soil which our good swords have
        won.
Still, like a spreading ulcer, which leech-craft may not cure,
Let your foul usance eat away the substance of the poor.
Still let your haggard debtors bear all their fathers bore ;
Still let your dens of torment be noisome as of yore ;
No fire when Tiber freezes ; no air in dog-star heat ;
And store of rods for free-born backs, and holes for free-born
        feet.
Heap heavier still the fetters ; bar closer still the grate ;
Patient as sheep we yield us up unto your cruel hate.

But, by the Shades beneath us, and by the Gods above,
Add not unto your cruel. hate your yet more cruel love!
Have ye not graceful ladies, whose spotless lineage springs
From Consuls, and High Pontiffs, and ancient Alban kings?
Ladies, who deign not on our paths to set their tender feet,
Who from their cars look down with scorn upon the wondering
    street,
Who in Corinthian mirrors their own proud smiles behold,
And breathe of Capuan odours, and shine with Spanish gold?
Then leave the poor Plebeian his single tie to life—
The sweet, sweet love of daughter, of sister, and of wife,
The gentle speech, the balm for all that his vexed soul endures,
The kiss, in which he half forgets even such a yoke as yours.
Still let the maiden's beauty swell the father's breast with pride;
Still let the bridegroom's arms infold an unpolluted bride.
Spare us the inexpiable wrong, the unutterable shame,
That turns the coward's heart to steel, the sluggard's blood to flame,
Lest, when our latest hope is fled, ye taste of our despair,
And learn by proof, in some wild hour, how much the wretched
    dare.'

   *     *     *     *     *     *     *
   *     *     *     *     *     *     *

  Straightway Virginius led the maid a little space aside,
To where the reeking shambles stood, piled up with horn and hide,
Close to yon low dark archway, where, in a crimson flood,
Leaps down to the great sewer the gurgling stream of blood.
Hard by, a flesher on a block had laid his whittle down;
Virginius caught the whittle up, and hid it in his gown.
And then his eyes grew very dim, and his throat began to swell,
And in a hoarse, changed voice he spake, 'Farewell, sweet
    child! Farewell!
Oh! how I loved my darling! Though stern I sometimes be,
To thee, thou know'st I was not so. Who could be so to thee?

And how my darling loved mo! How glad she was to hear
My footstep on the threshold when I came back last year!
And how she danced with pleasure to see my civic crown,
And took my sword, and hung it up, and brought me forth my
    gown!
Now, all those things are over—yes, all thy pretty ways,
Thy needlework, thy prattle, thy snatches of old lays;
And none will grieve when I go forth, or smile when I return,
Or watch beside the old man's bed, or weep upon his urn.
The house that was the happiest within the Roman walls,
The house that envied not the wealth of Capua's marble halls,
Now, for the brightness of thy smile, must have eternal gloom,
And for the music of thy voice, the silence of the tomb.
The time is come. See how he points his eager hand this way!
See how his eyes gloat on thy grief, like a kite's upon the prey!
With all his wit, he little deems, that, spurned, betrayed, bereft,
Thy father hath in his despair one fearful refuge left.
He little deems that in this hand I clutch what still can save
Thy gentle youth from taunts and blows, the portion of the slave;
Yea, and from nameless evil, that passeth taunt and blow—
Foul outrage which thou knowest not, which thou shalt never
    know.
Then clasp me round the neck once more, and give me one more
    kiss;
And now, mine own dear little girl, there is no way but this.'
With that he lifted high the steel, and smote her in the side,
And in her blood she sank to earth, and with one sob she died.

    Then, for a little moment, all people held their breath;
And through the crowded Forum was stillness as of death;
And in another moment brake forth from one and all
A cry as if the Volscians were coming o'er the wall.

Some with averted faces shrieking fled home amain ;
Some ran to call a leech ; and some ran to lift the slain :
Some felt her lips and little wrist, if life might there be found ;
And some tore up their garments fast, and strove to stanch the
    wound.
In vain they ran, and felt, and stanched ; for never truer blow
That good right arm had dealt in fight against a Volscian foe.


  When Appius Claudius saw that deed, he shuddered and sank
    down,
And hid his face some little space with the corner of his gown,
Till, with white lips and bloodshot eyes, Virginius tottered nigh,
And stood before the judgment-seat, and held the knife on high.
' Oh I dwellers in the nether gloom, avengers of the slain,
By this dear blood I cry to you, do right between us twain ;
And even as Appius Claudius hath dealt by me and mine,
Deal you by Appius Claudius and all the Claudian line ! '
So spake the slayer of his child, and turned, and went his way ;
But first he cast one haggard glance to where the body lay,
And writhed, and groaned a fearful groan, and then, with stead-
    fast feet,
Strode right across the market-place unto the Sacred Street.


  Then up sprang Appius Claudius : ' Stop him ; alive or dead !
Ten thousand pounds of copper to the man who brings his head.'
He looked upon his clients ; but none would work his will.
He looked upon his lictors ; but they trembled, and stood still.
And, as Virginius through the press his way in silence cleft,
Ever the mighty multitude fell back to right and left,
And he hath passed in safety unto his woeful home,
And there ta'en horse to tell the camp what deeds are done in
    Rome.

By this the flood of people was swollen from every side,
And streets and porches round were filled with that o'erflowing
    tide;
And close around the body gathered a little train
Of them that were the nearest and dearest to the slain.
They brought a bier, and hung it with many a cypress crown,
And gently they uplifted her, and gently laid her down.
The face of Appius Claudius wore the Claudian scowl and sneer,
And in the Claudian note he cried, ' What doth this rabble here ?
Have they no crafts to mind at home, that hitherward they stray ?
Ho ! lictors, clear the market-place, and fetch the corpse away !'
The voice of grief and fury till then had not been loud;
But a deep sullen murmur wandered among the crowd,
Like the moaning noise that goes before the whirlwind on the
    deep,
Or the growl of a fierce watch-dog but half-aroused from sleep.
But when the lictors at that word, tall yeomen all and strong,
Each with his axe and sheaf of twigs, went down into the throng,
Those old men say, who saw that day of sorrow and of sin,
That in the Roman Forum was never such a din.
The wailing, hooting, cursing, the howls of grief and hate,
Were heard beyond the Pincian Hill, beyond the Latin Gate.
But close around the body, where stood the little train
Of them that were the nearest and dearest to the slain,
No cries were there, but teeth set fast, low whispers and black
    frowns,
And breaking up of benches, and girding up of gowns.
'Twas well the lictors might not pierce to where the maiden lay,
Else surely had they been all twelve torn limb from limb that day.
Right glad they were to struggle back, blood streaming from
    their heads,
With axes all in splinters, and raiment all in shreds.

Then Appius Claudius gnawed his lip, and the blood left his cheek;
And thrice he beckoned with his hand, and thrice he strove to
    speak;
And thrice the tossing Forum set up a frightful yell;
' See, see, thou dog! what thou hast done; and hide thy shame
    in hell!
Thou that wouldst make our maidens slaves must first make
    slaves of men.
Tribunes! Hurrah for Tribunes! Down with the wicked Ten!'
And straightway, thick as hailstones, came whizzing through
    the air
Pebbles, and bricks, and potsherds, all round the curule chair:
And upon Appius Claudius great fear and trembling came;
For never was a Claudius yet brave against aught but shame.
Though the great houses love us not, we own, to do them right,
That the great houses, all save one, have borne them well in fight.
Still Caius of Corioli, his triumphs and his wrongs,
His vengeance and his mercy, live in our camp-fire songs.
Beneath the yoke of Furius oft have Gaul and Tuscan bowed;
And Rome may bear the pride of him of whom herself is proud.
But evermore a Claudius shrinks from a stricken field,
And changes colour like a maid at sight of sword and shield.
The Claudian triumphs all were won within the city towers;
The Claudian yoke was never pressed on any necks but ours.
A Cossus, like a wild cat, springs ever at the face;
A Fabius rushes like a boar against the shouting chase;
But the vile Claudian litter, raging with currish spite,
Still yelps and snaps at those who run, still runs from those who
    smite.
So now 'twas seen of Appius. When stones began to fly,
He shook, and crouched, and wrung his hands, and smote upon
    his thigh.

' Kind clients, honest lictors, stand by me in this fray !
Must I be torn in pieces ?  Home, home, the nearest way ! '
While yet he spake, and looked around with a bewildered stare,
Four sturdy lictors put their necks beneath the curule chair ;
And fourscore clients on the left, and fourscore on the right,
Arrayed themselves with swords and staves, and loins girt up for
    fight.
But, though without or staff or sword, so furious was the throng,
That scarce the train with might and main could bring their lord
    along.
Twelve times the crowd made at him ; five times they seized his
    gown;
Small chance was his to rise again, if once they got him down :
And sharper came the pelting ; and evermore the yell—
' Tribunes ! we will have Tribunes !'—rose with a louder swell :
And the chair tossed as tosses a bark with tattered sail
When raves the Adriatic beneath an eastern gale,
When the Calabrian sea-marks are lost in clouds of spume,
And the great Thunder-Cape has donned his veil of inky gloom.
One stone hit Appius in the mouth, and one beneath the ear ;
And ere he reached Mount Palatine, he swooned with pain and fear.
His cursed head, that he was wont to hold so high with pride,
Now, like a drunken man's, hung down, and swayed from side to
    side ;
And when his stout retainers had brought him to his door,
His face and neck were all one cake of filth and clotted gore.
As Appius Claudius was that day, so may his grandson be !
God send Rome one such other sight, and send me there to see !

    *     *     *     *     *     *     *

# THE PROPHECY OF CAPYS

# THE PROPHECY OF CAPYS.

It can hardly be necessary to remind any reader that according to the popular tradition, Romulus, after he had slain his grand-uncle Amulius, and restored his grandfather Numitor, determined to quit Alba, the hereditary domain of the Sylvian princes, and to found a new city. The Gods, it was added, vouchsafed the clearest signs of the favour with which they regarded the enterprise, and of the high destinies reserved for the young colony.

This event was likely to be a favourite theme of the old Latin minstrels. They would naturally attribute the project of Romulus to some divine intimation of the power and prosperity which it was decreed that his city should attain. They would probably introduce seers foretelling the victories of unborn Consuls and Dictators, and the last great victory would generally occupy the most conspicuous place in the prediction. There is nothing strange in the supposition that the poet who was employed to celebrate the first great triumph of the Romans over the Greeks might throw his song of exultation into this form.

The occasion was one likely to excite the strongest feelings of national pride. A great outrage had been followed by a great retribution. Seven years before this time, Lucius Posthumius Megellus, who sprung from one of the noblest houses of Rome, and had been thrice Consul, was sent ambassador to Tarentum, with charge to demand reparation for grievous injuries. The Tarentines gave him audience in their theatre, where he addressed them in such Greek as he could command, which, we may well believe, was not exactly such as Cineas would have spoken. An exquisite sense of the ridiculous belonged to the Greek character; and closely connected with this faculty was a strong propensity to flippancy and impertinence. When Posthumius placed an accent wrong, his hearers burst into a laugh. When he remonstrated, they hooted him, and called him barbarian; and at length hissed him off the stage as if he had been a bad actor. As the grave Roman retired, a buffoon who, from his constant drunkenness, was nicknamed the Pint-pot, came up with gestures of the grossest indecency, and bespattered the senatorial gown with filth. Posthumius turned round to the multitude, and held up the gown, as if appealing to the universal law of nations. The sight only increased the insolence of the Tarentines. They clapped their hands, and set up a shout of laughter which shook the theatre.

'Men of Tarentum,' said Posthumius, 'it will take not a little blood to wash this gown.'*

Rome, in consequence of this insult, declared war against the Tarentines. The Tarentines sought for allies beyond the Ionian Sea. Pyrrhus, king of Epirus, came to their help with a large army; and, for the first time, the two great nations of antiquity were fairly matched against each other.

The fame of Greece in arms, as well as in arts, was then at the height. Half a century earlier, the career of Alexander had excited the admiration and terror of all nations from the Ganges to the Pillars of Hercules. Royal houses, founded by Macedonian captains, still reigned at Antioch and Alexandria. That barbarian warriors, led by barbarian chiefs, should win a pitched battle against Greek valour guided by Greek science, seemed as incredible as it would now seem that the Burmese or the Siamese should, in the open plain, put to flight an equal number of the best English troops. The Tarentines were convinced that their countrymen were irresistible in war; and this conviction had emboldened them to treat with the grossest indignity one whom they regarded as the representative of an inferior race. Of the Greek generals then living, Pyrrhus was indisputably the first. Among the troops who were trained in the Greek discipline, his Epirotes ranked high. His

* Dion. Hal. De Legationibus.

expedition to Italy was a turning-point in the
history of the world. He found there a people
who, far inferior to the Athenians and Corinthians
in the fine arts, in the speculative sciences, and in
all the refinements of life, were the best soldiers on
the face of the earth. Their arms, their gradations
of rank, their order of battle, their method of
intrenchment, were all of Latian origin, and had
all been gradually brought near to perfection, not
by the study of foreign models, but by the genius
and experience of many generations of great native
commanders. The first words which broke from
the king, when his practised eye had surveyed
the Roman encampment, were full of meaning:—
'These barbarians,' he said, 'have nothing barbarous in their military arrangements.' He was
at first victorious; for his own talents were
superior to those of the captains who were opposed
to him; and the Romans were not prepared for
the onset of the elephants of the East, which were
then for the first time seen in Italy—moving mountains, with long snakes for hands.* But the
victories of the Epirotes were fiercely disputed,
dearly purchased, and altogether unprofitable. At
length, Manius Curius Dentatus, who had in his
first Consulship won two triumphs, was again
placed at the head of the Roman Commonwealth,

* *Anguimanus* is the old Latin epithet for an elephant.
Lucretius, ii. 538, v. 1302.

and sent to encounter the invaders. A great battle was fought near Beneventum. Pyrrhus was completely defeated. He repassed the sea; and the world learned, with amazement, that a people had been discovered, who, in fair fighting, were superior to the best troops that had been drilled on the system of Parmenio and Antigonus.

The conquerors had a good right to exult in their success; for their glory was all their own. They had not learned from their enemy how to conquer him. It was with their own national arms, and in their own national battle-array, that they had overcome weapons and tactics long believed to be invincible. The pilum and the broadsword had vanquished the Macedonian spear. The legion had broken the Macedonian phalanx. Even the elephants, when the surprise produced by their first appearance was over, could cause no disorder in the steady yet flexible battalions of Rome.

It is said by Florus, and may easily be believed, that the triumph far surpassed in magnificence any that Rome had previously seen. The only spoils which Papirius Cursor and Fabius Maximus could exhibit were flocks and herds, waggons of rude structure, and heaps of spears and helmets. But now, for the first time, the riches of Asia and the arts of Greece adorned a Roman pageant. Plate, fine stuffs, costly furniture, rare animals, exquisite paintings and sculptures, formed part of the pro-

cession.   At the banquet would be assembled a
crowd of warriors and statesmen, among whom
Manius Curius Dentatus would take the highest
room.   Caius Fabricius Luscinus, then, after two
Consulships and two triumphs, Censor of the
Commonwealth, would doubtless occupy a place of
honour at the board.   In situations less conspicuous probably lay some of those who were, a
few years later, the terror of Carthage; Caius
Duilius, the founder of the maritime greatness of
his country; Marcus Atilius Regulus, who owed
to defeat a renown far higher than that which he
had derived from his victories; and Caius Lutatius
Catulus, who, while suffering from a grievous
wound, fought the great battle of the Ægates, and
brought the first Punic war to a triumphant close.
It is impossible to recount the names of these
eminent citizens, without reflecting that they were
all, without exception, Plebeians, and would, but
for the ever-memorable struggle maintained by
Caius Licinius and Lucius Sextius, have been
doomed to hide in obscurity, or to waste in civil
broils, the capacity and energy which prevailed
against Pyrrhus and Hamilcar.

On such a day we may suppose that the patriotic
enthusiasm of a Latin poet would vent itself in
reiterated shouts of *Io triumphe*, such as were
uttered by Horace on a far less exciting occasion,
and in boasts resembling those which Virgil put

into the mouth of Anchises. The superiority of some foreign nations, and especially of the Greeks, in the lazy arts of peace, would be admitted with disdainful candour; but pre-eminence in all the qualities which fit a people to subdue and govern mankind would be claimed for the Romans.

The following lay belongs to the latest age of Latin ballad-poetry. Nævius and Livius Andronicus were probably among the children whose mothers held them up to see the chariot of Curius go by. The minstrel who sang on that day might possibly have lived to read the first hexameters of Ennius, and to see the first comedies of Plautus. His poem, as might be expected, shows a much wider acquaintance with the geography, manners, and productions of remote nations, than would have been found in compositions of the age of Camillus. But he troubles himself little about dates, and having heard travellers talk with admiration of the Colossus of Rhodes, and of the structures and gardens with which the Macedonian kings of Syria had embellished their residence on the banks of the Orontes, he has never thought of inquiring whether these things existed in the age of Romulus.

# THE PROPHECY OF CAPYS.

A LAY SUNG AT THE BANQUET IN THE CAPITOL, ON THE DAY
WHEREON MANIUS CURIUS DENTATUS, A SECOND TIME CONSUL,
TRIUMPHED OVER KING PYRRHUS AND THE TARENTINES, IN
THE YEAR OF THE CITY CCCCLXXIX.

---

I.

Now slain is King Amulius,
 Of the great Sylvian line,
Who reigned in Alba Longa,
 On the throne of Aventine.
Slain is the Pontiff Camers,
 Who spake the words of doom:
'The children to the Tiber;
 The mother to the tomb.'

II.

In Alba's lake no fisher
 His not to-day is flinging:
On the dark rind of Alba's oaks
 To-day no axe is ringing:
The yoke hangs o'er the manger:
 The scythe lies in the hay:
Through all the Alban villages
 No work is done to-day.

K

### III.

And every Alban burgher
  Hath donned his whitest gown :
And every head in Alba
  Weareth a poplar crown ;
And every Alban door-post
  With boughs and flowers is gay ;
For to-day the dead are living ;
  The lost are found to-day.

### IV.

They were doomed by a bloody king :
  They were doomed by a lying priest :
They were cast on the raging flood :
  They were tracked by the raging beast ,
Raging beast and raging flood
  Alike have spared the prey ;
And to-day the dead are living :
  The lost are found to-day.

### V.

The troubled river knew them,
  And smoothed his yellow foam,
And gently rocked the cradle
  That bore the fate of Rome.
The ravening she-wolf knew them,
  And licked them o'er and o'er,
And gave them of her own fierce milk,
  Rich with raw flesh and gore.

Twenty winters, twenty springs,
  Since then have rolled away;
And to-day the dead are living:
  The lost are found to-day.


### VI.

Blithe it was to see the twins,
  Right goodly youths and tall,
Marching from Alba Longa
  To their old grandsire's hall.
Along their path fresh garlands
  Are hung from tree to tree:
Before them stride the pipers,
  Piping a note of glee.


### VII.

On the right goes Romulus,
  With arms to the elbows red,
And in his hand a broadsword,
  And on the blade a head—
A head in an iron helmet,
  With horse-hair hanging down,
A shaggy head, a swarthy head,
  Fixed in a ghastly frown—
The head of King Amulius
  Of the great Sylvian line,
Who reigned in Alba Longa,
  On the throne of Aventine.

### VIII.

On tho loft side goes Remus,
  With wrists and fingers red,
And in his hand a boar-spear,
  And on tho point a head—
A wrinkled head and aged,
  With silver beard and hair,
And holy fillets round it,
  Such as the pontiffs wear—
The head of ancient Camers,
  Who spake tho words of doom:
'Tho children to the Tiber;
  Tho mother to the tomb.'

### IX.

Two and two behind tho twins
  Their trusty comrades go,
Four and forty valiant men,
  With club, and axe, and bow.
On each side every hamlet
  Pours forth its joyous crowd,
Shouting lads and baying dogs
  And children laughing loud,
And old men weeping fondly
  As Rhea's boys go by,
And maids who shriek to see tho heads,
  Yet, shrieking, press more nigh.

## I.

So they marched along the lake;
  They marched by fold and stall,
By corn-field and by vineyard,
  Unto the old man's hall.

## II.

In the hall-gate sate Capys,
  Capys, the sightless seer;
From head to foot he trembled
  As Romulus drew near.
And up stood stiff his thin white hair,
  And his blind eyes flashed fire:
'Hail! foster child of the wonderous nurse!
  Hail! son of the wonderous sire!

## XII.

'But thou—what dost thou here
  In the old man's peaceful hall?
What doth the eagle in the coop,
  The bison in the stall?
Our corn fills many a garner;
  Our vines clasp many a tree;
Our flocks are white on many a hill;
  But these are not for thee.

## XIII.

'For thee no treasure ripens
  In the Tartessian mine:

For thee no ship brings precious bales
  Across the Libyan brine:
Thou shalt not drink from amber;
  Thou shalt not rest on down;
Arabia shall not steep thy locks,
  Nor Sidon tinge thy gown.


### XIV.

' Leave gold and myrrh and jewels,
  Rich table and soft bed,
To them who of man's seed are born,
  Whom woman's milk have fed.
Thou wast not made for lucre,
  For pleasure, nor for rest;
Thou, that art sprung from the War-god's loins,
  And hast tugged at the she-wolf's breast.


### XV.

' From sunrise unto sunset
  All earth shall hear thy fame:
A glorious city thou shalt build,
  And name it by thy name:
And there, unquenched through ages,
  Like Vesta's sacred fire,
Shall live the spirit of thy nurse,
  The spirit of thy sire.


### XVI.

' The ox toils through the furrow,
  Obedient to the goad;

The patient ass, up flinty paths,
  Plods with his weary load :
With whine and bound the spaniel
  His master's whistle hears ;
And the sheep yields her patiently
  To the loud clashing shears.

### XVII.

' But thy nurse will hear no master;
  Thy nurse will bear no load;
And woe to them that shear her,
  And woe to them that goad !
When all the pack, loud baying,
  Her bloody lair surrounds,
She dies in silence, biting hard,
  Amidst the dying hounds.

### XVIII.

' Pomona loves the orchard ;
  And Liber loves the vine;
And Pales loves the straw-built shed
  Warm with the breath of kine ;
And Venus loves the whispers
  Of plighted youth and maid,
In April's ivory moonlight
  Beneath the chestnut shade.

### XIX.

' But thy father loves the clashing
  Of broadsword and of shield :
He loves to drink the steam that reeks
  From the fresh battle-field :

He smiles a smile more dreadful
  Than his own dreadful frown,
When he sees the thick black cloud of smoke
  Go up from the conquered town.


### XX.

' And such as is the War-god,
  The author of thy line,
And such as she who suckled thee,
  Even such be thou and thine.
Leave to the soft Campanian
  His baths and his perfumes ;
Leave to the sordid race of Tyre
  Their dyeing-vats and looms :
Leave to the sons of Carthage
  The rudder and the oar :
Leave to the Greek his marble Nymphs
  And scrolls of wordy lore.


### XXI.

' Thine, Roman, is the pilum :
  Roman, the sword is thine,
The even trench, the bristling mound,
  The legion's ordered line ;
And thine the wheels of triumph,
  Which with their laurelled train
Move slowly up the shouting streets
  To Jove's eternal fane.

#### XXII.

' Beneath thy yoke the Volscian
    Shall vail his lofty brow :
Soft Capua's curled revellers
    Before thy chairs shall bow :
The Lucumoes of Arnus
    Shall quake thy rods to see ;
And the proud Samnite's heart of steel
    Shall yield to only thee.

#### XXIII.

' The Gaul shall come against thee
    From the land of snow and night :
Thou shalt give his fair-haired armies
    To the raven and the kite.

#### XXIV.

' The Greek shall come against thee,
    The conqueror of the East.
Beside him stalks to battle
    The huge earth-shaking beast,
The beast on whom the castle
    With all its guards doth stand,
The beast who hath between his eyes
    The serpent for a hand.
First march the bold Epirotes,
    Wedged close with shield and spear ;
And the ranks of false Tarentum
    Are glittering in the rear.

### XXV.

'The ranks of false Tarentum
   Like hunted sheep shall fly:
In vain the bold Epirotes
   Shall round their standards die:
And Apennine's grey vultures
   Shall have a noble feast
On the fat and the eyes
   Of the huge earth-shaking beast.

### XXVI.

'Hurrah! for the good weapons
   That keep the War-god's land.
Hurrah! for Rome's stout pilum
   In a stout Roman hand.
Hurrah! for Rome's short broadsword,
   That through the thick array
Of levelled spears and serried shields
   Hews deep its gory way.

### XXVII.

'Hurrah! for the great triumph
   That stretches many a mile.
Hurrah! for the wan captives
   That pass in endless file.
Ho! bold Epirotes, whither
   Hath the Red King ta'en flight?
Ho! dogs of false Tarentum,
   Is not the gown washed white?

### XXVIII.

'Hurrah! for the great triumph
　That stretches many a mile.
Hurrah! for tho rich dye of Tyro,
　And the fine web of Nile,
The helmets gay with plumage
　Torn from the pheasant's wings,
The belts set thick with starry gems
　That shone on Indian kings,
The urns of massy silver,
　The goblets rough with gold,
The many-coloured tablets bright
　With loves and wars of old,
The stone that breathes and struggles,
　Tho brass that seems to speak;—
Such cunning they who dwell on high
　Have given unto the Greek.

### XXIX.

Hurrah! for Manius Curius,
　The bravest son of Rome,
Thrice in utmost need sent forth,
　Thrice drawn in triumph home.
Weave, weave, for Manius Curius
　The third embroidered gown:
Make ready the third lofty car,
　And twine the third green crown;
And yoke the steeds of Rosea
　With necks like a bended bow,
And deck the bull, Mevania's bull,
　The bull as white as snow.

### XXX.

'Blest and thrice blest the Roman
  Who sees Rome's brightest day,
Who sees that long victorious pomp
  Wind down the Sacred Way,
And through the bellowing Forum,
  And round the Suppliant's Grove,
Up to the everlasting gates
  Of Capitolian Jove.

### XXXI.

'Then where, o'er two bright havens,
  The towers of Corinth frown;
Where the gigantic King of Day
  On his own Rhodes looks down;
Where soft Orontes murmurs
  Beneath the laurel shades;
Where Nile reflects the endless length
  Of dark-red colonnades;
Where in the still deep water,
  Sheltered from waves and blasts,
Bristles the dusky forest
  Of Byrsa's thousand masts;
Where fur-clad hunters wander
  Amidst the northern ice;
Where through the sand of morning-land
  The camel bears the spice;
Where Atlas flings his shadow
  Far o'er the western foam,
Shall be great fear on all who hear
  The mighty name of Rome.'

# IVRY:

## A SONG OF THE HUGUENOTS.

# IVRY.

Now glory to the Lord of Hosts, from whom all glories are!
And glory to our Sovereign Liege, King Henry of Navarro!
Now let there be the merry sound of music and of dance,
Through thy corn-fields green, and sunny vines, oh pleasant land
 of France!
And thou, Rochelle, our own Rochelle, proud city of the waters,
Again let rapture light the eyes of all thy mourning daughters.
As thou wert constant in our ills, be joyous in our joy,
For cold, and stiff, and still are they who wrought thy walls annoy.
Hurrah! Hurrah! a single field hath turned the chance of war,
Hurrah! Hurrah! for Ivry, and Henry of Navarro.

Oh! how our hearts were beating, when, at the dawn of day,
We saw the army of the League drawn out in long array;
With all its priest-led citizens, and all its rebel peers,
And Appenzel's stout infantry, and Egmont's Flemish spears.
There rode the brood of false Lorraine, the curses of our land;
And dark Mayenne was in the midst, a truncheon in his hand:
And, as we looked on them, we thought of Seine's empurpled flood,
And good Coligni's hoary hair all dabbled with his blood;
And we cried unto the living God, who rules the fate of war,
To fight for His own holy name, and Henry of Navarre.

The King is come to marshal us, in all his armour drest,
And he has bound a snow-white plume upon his gallant crest.

He looked upon his people, and a tear was in his eye;
He looked upon the traitors, and his glance was stern and high.
Right graciously he smiled on us, as rolled from wing to wing,
Down all our line, a deafening shout, 'God save our Lord the
    King!'
'And if my standard-bearer fall, as fall full well he may,
'For never saw I promise yet of such a bloody fray,
'Press where ye see my white plume shine, amidst the ranks of
    war,
'And be your oriflamme to-day the helmet of Navarre.'

Hurrah! the foes are moving. Hark to the mingled din
Of fife, and steed, and tramp, and drum, and roaring culverin.
The fiery Duke is pricking fast across Saint André's plain,
With all the hireling chivalry of Guelders and Almayne.
Now by the lips of those ye love, fair gentlemen of France,
Charge for the golden lilies,—upon them with the lance.
A thousand spurs are striking deep, a thousand spears in rest,
A thousand knights are pressing close behind the snow-white
    crest;
And in they burst, and on they rushed, while, like a guiding star,
Amidst the thickest carnage blazed the helmet of Navarre.

Now, God be praised, the day is ours. Mayenne hath turned his
    rein.
D'Aumale hath cried for quarter. The Flemish count is slain.
Their ranks are breaking like thin clouds before a Biscay gale;
The field is heaped with bleeding steeds, and flags, and cloven mail.
And then we thought on vengeance, and, all along our van,
'Remember St. Bartholomew,' was passed from man to man.
But out spake gentle Henry, 'No Frenchman is my foe:
'Down, down with every foreigner, but let your brethren go.'

Oh! was there ever such a knight, in friendship or in war,
As our Sovereign Lord, King Henry, the soldier of Navarre?

Right well fought all the Frenchmen who fought for France to-day:
And many a lordly banner God gave them for a prey.
But we of the religion have borne us best in fight;
And the good Lord of Rosny has ta'en the cornet white.
Our own true Maximilian the cornet white hath ta'en,
The cornet white with crosses black, the flag of false Lorraine.
Up with it high; unfurl it wide; that all the host may know
How God hath humbled the proud house which wrought His
    church such woe.
Then on the ground, while trumpets sound their loudest point of
    war,
Fling the red shreds, a footcloth meet for Henry of Navarre.

Ho! maidens of Vienna; Ho! matrons of Lucerne;
Weep, weep, and rend your hair for those who never shall return.
Ho! Philip, send, for charity, thy Mexican pistoles,
That Antwerp monks may sing a mass for thy poor spearmen's
    souls.
Ho! gallant nobles of the League, look that your arms be bright;
Ho! burghers of Saint Genevieve, keep watch and ward to-night.
For our God hath crushed the tyrant, our God hath raised the
    slave,
And mocked the counsel of the wise, and the valour of the brave.
Then glory to His holy name, from whom all glories are;
And glory to our Sovereign Lord, King Henry of Navarre.

1824.

# THE ARMADA:

## A FRAGMENT.

# THE ARMADA.

Attend, all ye who list to hear our noble England's praise;
I tell of the thrice famous deeds she wrought in ancient days,
When that great fleet invincible against her bore in vain
The richest spoils of Mexico, the stoutest hearts of Spain.

It was about the lovely close of a warm summer day,
There came a gallant merchant-ship full sail to Plymouth Bay;
Her crew hath seen Castile's black fleet, beyond Aurigny's isle,
At earliest twilight, on the waves lie heaving many a mile.
At sunrise she escaped their van, by God's especial grace;
And the tall Pinta, till the noon, had held her close in chase.
Forthwith a guard at every gun was placed along the wall;
The beacon blazed upon the roof of Edgecumbe's lofty hall;
Many a light fishing-bark put out to pry along the coast,
And with loose rein and bloody spur rode inland many a post.
With his white hair unbonneted, the stout old sheriff comes;
Behind him march the halberdiers; before him sound the drums;
His yeomen round the market cross make clear an ample space;
For there behoves him to set up the standard of Her Grace.
And haughtily the trumpets peal, and gaily dance the bells,
As slow upon the labouring wind the royal blazon swells.
Look how the Lion of the sea lifts up his ancient crown,
And underneath his deadly paw treads the gay lilies down.
So stalked he when he turned to flight, on that famed Picard field,
Bohemia's plume, and Genoa's bow, and Cæsar's eagle shield.

So glared he when at Agincourt in wrath he turned to bay,
And crushed and torn beneath his claws the princely hunters lay.
Ho ! strike the flagstaff deep, Sir Knight : ho ! scatter flowers,
    fair maids :
Ho ! gunners, fire a loud salute : ho ! gallants, draw your blades :
Then sun, shine on her joyously ; ye breezes, waft her wide ;
Our glorious SEMPER EADEM, the banner of our pride.

    The freshening breeze of eve unfurled that banner's massy fold ;
The parting gleam of sunshine kissed that haughty scroll of gold ;
Night sank upon the dusky beach, and on the purple sea,
Such night in England ne'er had been, nor e'er again shall be.
From Eddystone to Berwick bounds, from Lynn to Milford Bay,
That time of slumber was as bright and busy as the day ;
For swift to east and swift to west the ghastly war-flame spread,
High on St. Michael's Mount it shone : it shone on Beachy
    Head.
Far on the deep the Spaniard saw, along each southern shire,
Cape beyond cape, in endless range, those twinkling points of fire.
The fisher left his skiff to rock on Tamar's glittering waves :
The rugged miners poured to war from Mendip's sunless caves :
O'er Longleat's towers, o'er Cranbourne's oaks, the fiery herald
    flew :
He roused the shepherds of Stonehenge, the rangers of Beaulieu.
Right sharp and quick the bells all night rang out from Bristol
    town,
And ere the day three hundred horse had met on Clifton down ;
The sentinel on Whitehall gate looked forth into the night,
And saw o'erhanging Richmond Hill the streak of blood-red light.
Then bugle's note and cannon's roar the deathlike silence broke,
And with one start, and with one cry, the royal city woke.
At once on all her stately gates arose the answering fires ;
At once the wild alarum clashed from all her reeling spires ;

From all the batteries of the Tower pealed loud the voice of
    fear;
And all the thousand masts of Thames sent back a louder cheer:
And from the furthest wards was heard the rush of hurrying feet,
And the broad streams of pikes and flags rushed down each
    roaring street;
And broader still became the blaze, and louder still the din,
As fast from every village round the horse came spurring in:
And eastward straight from wild Blackheath the warlike errand
    went,
And roused in many an ancient hall the gallant squires of Kent.
Southward from Surrey's pleasant hills flew those bright couriers
    forth;
High on bleak Hampstead's swarthy moor they started for the
    north;
And on, and on, without a pause, untired they bounded still:
All night from tower to tower they sprang; they sprang from
    hill to hill:
Till the proud peak unfurled the flag o'er Darwin's rocky dales,
Till like volcanoes flared to heaven the stormy hills of Wales,
Till twelve fair counties saw the blaze on Malvern's lonely height,
Till streamed in crimson on the wind the Wrekin's crest of light,
Till broad and fierce the star came forth on Ely's stately fane,
And tower and hamlet rose in arms o'er all the boundless plain;
Till Belvoir's lordly terraces the sign to Lincoln sent,
And Lincoln sped the message on o'er the wide vale of Trent;
Till Skiddaw saw the fire that burned on Gaunt's embattled pile,
And the red glare on Skiddaw roused the burghers of Carlisle.

    &bull;      &bull;      &bull;      &bull;

    1832.

NOVEMBER 1874.

# GENERAL LIST OF WORKS

### PUBLISHED BY

## Messrs. LONGMANS, GREEN, and CO.

### PATERNOSTER ROW, LONDON.

---

### *History, Politics, Historical Memoirs, &c.*

**JOURNAL of the REIGNS of KING GEORGE IV. and KING WILLIAM IV.** By the late CHARLES C. F. GREVILLE, Esq. Clerk of the Council to those Sovereigns. Edited by HENRY REEVE, Registrar of the Privy Council. 3 vols. 8vo. 36s.

**RECOLLECTIONS and SUGGESTIONS of PUBLIC LIFE, 1813-1873.** By JOHN Earl RUSSELL. 1 vol. 8vo. [*Nearly ready.*]

**The HISTORY of ENGLAND** from the Fall of Wolsey to the Defeat of the Spanish Armada. By JAMES ANTHONY FROUDE, M.A. late Fellow of Exeter College, Oxford.
> LIBRARY EDITION, Twelve Volumes, 8vo. price £8. 18s.
> CABINET EDITION, Twelve Volumes, crown 8vo. price 72s.

**The ENGLISH in IRELAND in the EIGHTEENTH CENTURY.** By JAMES ANTHONY FROUDE, M.A. late Fellow of Exeter College, Oxford. 3 vols. 8vo. price 48s.

**ESTIMATES of the ENGLISH KINGS from WILLIAM the CON-QUEROR to GEORGE III.** By J. LANGTON SANFORD. Crown 8vo. 12s. 6d.

**The HISTORY of ENGLAND** from the Accession of James II. By Lord MACAULAY.
> STUDENT'S EDITION, 2 vols. crown 8vo. 12s.
> PEOPLE'S EDITION, 4 vols. crown 8vo. 16s.
> CABINET EDITION, 8 vols. post 8vo. 48s.
> LIBRARY EDITION, 5 vols. 8vo. £4.

**LORD MACAULAY'S WORKS.** Complete and Uniform Library Edition. Edited by his Sister, Lady TREVELYAN. 8 vols. 8vo. with Portrait, price £5. 5s. cloth, or £8. 8s. bound in tree-calf by Rivière.

**On PARLIAMENTARY GOVERNMENT in ENGLAND; its Origin, Development, and Practical Operation.** By ALPHEUS TODD, Librarian of the Legislative Assembly of Canada. 2 vols. 8vo. price £1. 17s.

**The CONSTITUTIONAL HISTORY of ENGLAND, since the Accession of George III. 1760—1860.** By Sir THOMAS ERSKINE MAY, C.B. The Fourth Edition, thoroughly revised. 3 vols. crown 8vo. price 18s.

**DEMOCRACY in EUROPE; a History.** By Sir THOMAS ERSKINE MAY, K.C.B. 2 vols. 8vo. [*In the press.*]

A

The **ENGLISH GOVERNMENT** and **CONSTITUTION** from Henry VII. to the Present Time. By JOHN Earl RUSSELL, K.G. Fcp. 8vo. 3s. 6d.

The **OXFORD REFORMERS** — John Colet, Erasmus, and Thomas More; being a History of their Fellow-work. By FREDERIC SEEBOHM. Second Edition, enlarged. 8vo. 14s.

**LECTURES** on the **HISTORY** of **ENGLAND**, from the Earliest Times to the Death of King Edward II. By WILLIAM LONGMAN, F.S.A. With Maps and Illustrations. 8vo. 15s.

The **HISTORY** of the **LIFE** and **TIMES** of **EDWARD** the **THIRD**. By WILLIAM LONGMAN, F.S.A. With 9 Maps, 8 Plates, and 16 Woodcuts. 2 vols. 8vo. 28s.

**INTRODUCTORY LECTURES** on **MODERN HISTORY**. Delivered in Lent Term, 1842; with the Inaugural Lecture delivered in December 1841: By the Rev. THOMAS ARNOLD, D.D. 8vo. price 7s. 6d.

**WATERLOO LECTURES**; a Study of the Campaign of 1815. By Colonel CHARLES C. CHESNEY, R.E. Third Edition. 8vo. with Map, 10s. 6d.

**HISTORY** of **ENGLAND** under the **DUKE** of **BUCKINGHAM** and CHARLES the FIRST, 1624-1628. By SAMUEL RAWSON GARDINER, late Student of Ch. Ch. 2 vols. 8vo. [*In the press.*]

The **SIXTH ORIENTAL MONARCHY**; or, the Geography, History, and Antiquities of Parthia. By GEORGE RAWLINSON, M.A. Professor of Ancient History in the University of Oxford. Maps and Illustrations. 8vo. 16s.

The **SEVENTH GREAT ORIENTAL MONARCHY**; or, a History of the Sassanians; with Notices, Geographical and Antiquarian. By G. RAWLINSON, M.A. Professor of Ancient History in the University of Oxford. 8vo. with Maps and Illustrations. [*In the press.*]

A **HISTORY** of **GREECE**. By the Rev. GEORGE W. COX, M.A. late Scholar of Trinity College, Oxford. VOLS. I. & II. (to the Close of the Peloponnesian War) 8vo. with Maps and Plans, 36s.

The **HISTORY OF GREECE**. By Rev. CONNOP THIRLWALL, D.D. late Bishop of St. David's. 8 vols. fcp. 8vo. 28s.

**GREEK HISTORY** from Themistocles to Alexander, in a Series of Lives from Plutarch. Revised and arranged by A. H. CLOUGH. New Edition. Fcp. with 44 Woodcuts, 6s.

The **TALE** of the **GREAT PERSIAN WAR**, from the Histories of Herodotus. By GEORGE W. COX, M.A. New Edition. Fcp. 3s. 6d.

The **HISTORY** of **ROME**. By WILLIAM IHNE. VOLS. I. and II. 8vo. price 30s. VOLS. III. and IV. preparing for publication.

**HISTORY** of the **ROMANS** under the **EMPIRE**. By the Very Rev. C. MERIVALE, D.C.L. Dean of Ely. 8 vols. post 8vo. 48s.

The **FALL** of the **ROMAN REPUBLIC**; a Short History of the Last Century of the Commonwealth. By the same Author. 12mo. 7s. 6d.

The **STUDENT'S MANUAL** of the **HISTORY** of **INDIA**, from the Earliest Period to the Present. By Colonel MEADOWS TAYLOR, M.R.A.S. M.R.I.A. Second Thousand. Crown 8vo. with Maps, 7s. 6d.

The **HISTORY** of **INDIA**, from the Earliest Period to the close of Lord Dalhousie's Administration. By J. C. MARSHMAN. 3 vols. crown 8vo. 22s. 6d.

**INDIAN POLITY**; a View of the System of Administration in India. By Lieutenant-Colonel GEORGE CHESNEY, Fellow of the University of Calcutta. New Edition, revised; with Map. 8vo. price 21s.

The **IMPERIAL** and **COLONIAL CONSTITUTIONS** of the **BRITANNIC EMPIRE**, including INDIAN INSTITUTIONS. By Sir EDWARD CREASY, M.A. With 6 Maps. 8vo. price 15s.

The **HISTORY of PERSIA** and its **PRESENT POLITICAL SITUATION**; with Abstracts of all Treaties and Conventions between Persia and England, and of the Convention with Baron Reuter. By CLEMENTS R. MARKHAM, C.B. F.R.S. 8vo. with Map, 21s.

**REALITIES of IRISH LIFE**. By W. STEUART TRENCH, late Land Agent in Ireland to the Marquess of Lansdowne, the Marquess of Bath, and Lord Digby. Cheaper Edition. Crown 8vo. price 2s. 6d.

**CRITICAL** and **HISTORICAL ESSAYS** contributed to the *Edinburgh Review*. By the Right Hon. LORD MACAULAY.

CHEAP EDITION, authorised and complete. Crown 8vo. 3s. 6d.

| | |
|---|---|
| CABINET EDITION, 4 vols. post 8vo. 24s. | LIBRARY EDITION, 3 vols. 8vo. 36s. |
| PEOPLE'S EDITION, 2 vols. crown 8vo. 8s. | STUDENT'S EDITION, 1 vol. cr. 8vo. 6s. |

**HISTORY of EUROPEAN MORALS**, from Augustus to Charlemagne By W. E. H. LECKY, M.A. Second Edition. 2 vols. 8vo. price 28s.

**HISTORY of the RISE** and **INFLUENCE** of the **SPIRIT of RATIONALISM** in EUROPE. By W. E. H. LECKY, M.A. Cabinet Edition, being the Fourth. 2 vols. crown 8vo. price 16s.

The **HISTORY of PHILOSOPHY**, from Thales to Comte. By GEORGE HENRY LEWES. Fourth Edition. 2 vols. 8vo. 32s.

The **HISTORY of the PELOPONNESIAN WAR**. By THUCYDIDES. Translated by R. CRAWLEY, Fellow of Worcester College, Oxford. 8vo. 21s.

The **MYTHOLOGY of the ARYAN NATIONS**. By GEORGE W. Cox, M.A. late Scholar of Trinity College, Oxford, 2 vols. 8vo. 28s.

**HISTORY of CIVILISATION** in England and France, Spain and Scotland. By HENRY THOMAS BUCKLE. New Edition of the entire Work, with a complete INDEX. 3 vols. crown 8vo. 21s.

**SKETCH of the HISTORY of the CHURCH of ENGLAND** to the Revolution of 1688. By the Right Rev. T. V. SHORT, D.D. Lord Bishop of St. Asaph. Eighth Edition. Crown 8vo. 7s. 6d.

**HISTORY of the EARLY CHURCH**, from the First Preaching of the Gospel to the Council of Nicæa, A.D. 325. By Miss SEWELL. Fcp. 8vo. 4s. 6d.

**MAUNDER'S HISTORICAL TREASURY**; General Introductory Outlines of Universal History, and a series of Separate Histories. Latest Edition, revised by the Rev. G. W. Cox, M.A. Fcp. 8vo. 6s. cloth, or 10s. calf.

**CATES'** and **WOODWARD'S ENCYCLOPÆDIA of CHRONOLOGY**, HISTORICAL and BIOGRAPHICAL; comprising the Dates of all the Great Events of History, including Treaties, Alliances, Wars, Battles, &c.; Incidents in the Lives of Eminent Men and their Works, Scientific and Geographical Discoveries, Mechanical Inventions, and Social Improvements. 8vo. price 42s.

The **FRENCH REVOLUTION** and **FIRST EMPIRE**; an Historical Sketch. By WILLIAM O'CONNOR MORRIS, sometime Scholar of Oriel College, Oxford. With 2 Coloured Maps. Post 8vo. 7s. 6d.

The **HISTORICAL GEOGRAPHY of EUROPE**. By E. A. FREEMAN, D.C.L. late Fellow of Trinity College, Oxford. 8vo. Maps. [*In the press.*

A 2

**EPOCHS of HISTORY**; a Series of Books treating of the History of England and Europe at successive Epochs subsequent to the Christian Era. Edited by EDWARD E. MORRIS, M.A. of Lincoln College, Oxford. The three following are now ready :—

**The Era of the Protestant Revolution.** By F. SEEBOHM. With 4 Maps and 12 Diagrams. Fcp. 8vo. 2s. 6d.

**The Crusades.** By the Rev. G. W. Cox, M.A. late Scholar of Trinity College, Oxford. With Coloured Map. Fcp. 8vo. 2s. 6d.

**The Thirty Years' War, 1618-1648.** By SAMUEL RAWSON GARDINER, late Student of Christ Church. With Coloured Map. Fcp. 8vo. 2s. 6d.

**The Houses of Lancaster and York;** with the Conquest and Loss of France. By JAMES GAIRDNER, of the Public Record Office. With Maps. Fcp. 8vo. 2s. 6d.

**Edward the Third.** By the Rev. W. WARBURTON, M.A. late Fellow of All Souls College, Oxford. With Maps. Fcp. 8vo. 2s. 6d.

## Biographical Works.

**AUTOBIOGRAPHY.** By JOHN STUART MILL. 8vo. price 7s. 6d.

**The LIFE of NAPOLEON III.** derived from State Records, Unpublished Family Correspondence, and Personal Testimony. By BLANCHARD JERROLD. In Four Volumes. VOL. I. with 3 Portraits engraved on Steel and 9 Facsimiles. 8vo. price 18s. VOL. II. is in the press.

**LIFE and CORRESPONDENCE of RICHARD WHATELY, D.D.** Late Archbishop of Dublin. By E. JANE WHATELY. New Edition, in 1 vol. crown 8vo.                                                [*In the press.*

**LIFE and LETTERS of Sir GILBERT ELLIOT, First EARL of MINTO.** Edited by the COUNTESS of MINTO. 3 vols. 8vo. 31s. 6d.

**MEMOIR of THOMAS FIRST LORD DENMAN,** formerly Lord Chief Justice of England. By Sir JOSEPH ARNOULD, D.A. K.B. late Judge of the High Court of Bombay. With 2 Portraits. 2 vols. 8vo. 52s.

**ESSAYS in MODERN MILITARY BIOGRAPHY.** By CHARLES CORNWALLIS CHESNEY, Lieutenant-Colonel in the Royal Engineers. 8vo. 12s. 6d.

**ISAAC CASAUBON, 1559-1614.** By MARK PATTISON, Rector of Lincoln College, Oxford. 8vo.                              [*In the press.*

**BIOGRAPHICAL and CRITICAL ESSAYS,** reprinted from Reviews, with Additions and Corrections. Second Edition of the Second Series. By A. HAYWARD, Q.C. 2 vols. 8vo. price 28s. THIRD SERIES, in 1 vol. 8vo. price 14s.

**The LIFE of LLOYD, FIRST LORD KENYON, LORD CHIEF JUSTICE of ENGLAND.** By the Hon. GEORGE T. KENYON, M.A. of Ch. Ch. Oxford. With Portraits. 8vo. price 14s.

**MEMOIR of GEORGE EDWARD LYNCH COTTON, D.D.** Bishop of Calcutta and Metropolitan. With Selections from his Journals and Correspondence. Edited by Mrs. COTTON. Crown 8vo. 7s. 6d.

**LIFE of ALEXANDER VON HUMBOLDT.** Compiled in Commemoration of the Centenary of his Birth, and edited by Professor KARL BRUHNS; translated by JANE and CAROLINE LASSELL, with 3 Portraits. 2 vols. 8vo. 36s.

**LORD GEORGE BENTINCK;** a Political Biography. By the Right Hon. BENJAMIN DISRAELI, M.P. Crown 8vo. price 6s.

The **LIFE OF ISAMBARD KINGDOM BRUNEL, Civil Engineer.** By ISAMBARD BRUNEL, B.C.L. With Portrait, Plates, and Woodcuts. 8vo. 21s.

**RECOLLECTIONS of PAST LIFE.** By Sir HENRY HOLLAND, Bart. M.D. F.R.S. late Physician-in-Ordinary to the Queen. Third Edition. Post 8vo. price 10s. 6d.

The **LIFE and LETTERS of the Rev. SYDNEY SMITH.** Edited by his Daughter, Lady HOLLAND, and Mrs. AUSTIN. Crown 8vo. price 7s. 6d.

**LEADERS of PUBLIC OPINION in IRELAND;** Swift, Flood, Grattan, and O'Connell. By W. E. H. LECKY, M.A. New Edition, revised and enlarged. Crown 8vo. price 7s. 6d.

**DICTIONARY of GENERAL BIOGRAPHY;** containing Concise Memoirs and Notices of the most Eminent Persons of all Countries, from the Earliest Ages to the Present Time. Edited by W. L. R. CATES. 8vo. 21s.

**LIFE of the DUKE of WELLINGTON.** By the Rev. G. R. GLEIG, M.A. Popular Edition, carefully revised; with copious Additions. Crown 8vo. with Portrait, 5s.

**FELIX MENDELSSOHN'S LETTERS** from *Italy and Switzerland,* and *Letters from 1833 to 1847,* translated by Lady WALLACE. New Edition, with Portrait. 2 vols. crown 8vo. 5s. each.

**MEMOIRS of SIR HENRY HAVELOCK, K.C.B.** By JOHN CLARK MARSHMAN. Cabinet Edition, with Portrait. Crown 8vo. price 3s. 6d.

**VICISSITUDES of FAMILIES.** By Sir J. BERNARD BURKE, C.B. Ulster King of Arms. New Edition, remodelled and enlarged. 2 vols. crown 8vo. 21s.

The **RISE of GREAT FAMILIES,** other Essays and Stories. By Sir J. BERNARD BURKE, C.B. Ulster King of Arms. Crown 8vo. price 12s. 6d.

**ESSAYS in ECCLESIASTICAL BIOGRAPHY.** By the Right Hon. Sir J. STEPHEN, LL.D. Cabinet Edition. Crown 8vo. 7s. 6d.

**MAUNDER'S BIOGRAPHICAL TREASURY.** Latest Edition, reconstructed, thoroughly revised, and in great part rewritten; with 1,000 additional Memoirs and Notices, by W. L. R. CATES. Fcp. 8vo. 6s. cloth; 10s. calf.

**LETTERS and LIFE of FRANCIS BACON,** including all his Occasional Works. Collected and edited, with a Commentary, by J. SPEDDING, Trin. Coll. Cantab. Complete in 7 vols. 8vo. £4. 4s.

## Criticism, Philosophy, Polity, &c.

A **SYSTEMATIC VIEW of the SCIENCE of JURISPRUDENCE.** By SHELDON AMOS, M.A. Professor of Jurisprudence to the Inns of Court, London. 8vo. price 18s.

A **PRIMER of the ENGLISH CONSTITUTION and GOVERNMENT.** By SHELDON AMOS, M.A. Professor of Jurisprudence to the Inns of Court. New Edition, revised. Post 8vo. [*In the press.*

The **INSTITUTES of JUSTINIAN**; with English Introduction, Translation and Notes. By T. C. SANDARS, M.A. Sixth Edition. 8vo. 18s.

**SOCRATES and the SOCRATIC SCHOOLS.** Translated from the German of Dr. E. ZELLER, with the Author's approval, by the Rev. OSWALD J. REICHEL, M.A. Crown 8vo. 8s. 6d.

The **STOICS, EPICUREANS, and SCEPTICS.** Translated from the German of Dr. E. ZELLER, with the Author's approval, by OSWALD J. REICHEL, M.A. Crown 8vo. price 14s.

The **ETHICS of ARISTOTLE**, illustrated with Essays and Notes, By Sir A. GRANT, Bart. M.A. LL.D. Third Edition, revised and partly rewritten. *[In the press.*

The **POLITICS of ARISTOTLE;** Greek Text, with English Notes. By RICHARD CONGREVE, M.A. New Edition, revised. 8vo. 18s.

The **NICOMACHEAN ETHICS of ARISTOTLE** newly translated into English. By R. WILLIAMS, B.A. Fellow and late Lecturer of Merton College, and sometime Student of Christ Church, Oxford. 8vo. 12s.

**ELEMENTS of LOGIC.** By R. WHATELY, D.D. late Archbishop of Dublin. New Edition. 8vo. 10s. 6d. crown 8vo. 4s. 6d.

**Elements of Rhetoric.** By the same Author. New Edition. 8vo. 10s. 6d. crown 8vo. 4s. 6d.

**English Synonymes.** By E. JANE WHATELY. Edited by Archbishop WHATELY. Fifth Edition. Fcp. 8vo. price 3s.

**DEMOCRACY in AMERICA.** By ALEXIS DE TOCQUEVILLE. Translated by HENRY REEVE, C.B., D.C.L., Corresponding Member of the Institute of France. New Edition, in two vols. post 8vo. *[In the press.*

**POLITICAL PROBLEMS.** Reprinted chiefly from the *Fortnightly Review*, revised, and with New Essays. By FREDERIC HARRISON, of Lincoln's Inn. 1 vol. 8vo. *[In the press.*

**THE SYSTEM of POSITIVE POLITY, or TREATISE upon SOCI-** OLOGY, of AUGUSTE COMTE, Author of the System of Positive Philosophy. Translated from the Paris Edition of 1851-1854, and furnished with Analytical Tables of Contents. In Four Volumes, 8vo. to be published separately:— *[In the press.*

VOL. I. The General View of Positive Polity and its Philosophical Basis. Translated by J. H. BRIDGES, M.D.

VOL. II. The Social Statics, or the Abstract Laws of Human Order. Translated by F. HARRISON, M.A.

VOL. III. The Social Dynamics, or the General Laws of Human Progress (the Philosophy of History). Translated by E. S. BEESLY, M.A.

VOL. IV. The Synthesis of the Future of Mankind. Translated by R. CONGREVE, M.A.

**BACON'S ESSAYS with ANNOTATIONS.** By R. WHATELY, D.D. late Archbishop of Dublin. New Edition, 8vo. price 10s. 6d.

**LORD BACON'S WORKS,** collected and edited by J. SPEDDING, M.A. R. L. ELLIS, M.A. and D. D. HEATH. 7 vols. 8vo. price £3. 13s. 6d.

**ESSAYS CRITICAL and NARRATIVE.** By WILLIAM FORSYTH, Q.C. LL.D. M.P. for Marylebone; Author of 'The Life of Cicero,' &c. 8vo. 16s.

The **SUBJECTION** of **WOMEN**. By JOHN STUART MILL. New Edition. Post 8vo. 5s.

On **REPRESENTATIVE GOVERNMENT**. By JOHN STUART MILL. Crown 8vo. price 2s.

On **LIBERTY**. By JOHN STUART MILL. New Edition. Post 8vo. 7s. 6d. Crown 8vo. price 1s. 4d.

**PRINCIPLES of POLITICAL ECONOMY.** By the same Author. Seventh Edition. 2 vols. 8vo. 30s. Or in 1 vol. crown 8vo. price 5s.

**ESSAYS on SOME UNSETTLED QUESTIONS of POLITICAL** ECONOMY. By JOHN STUART MILL. Second Edition. 8vo. 6s. 6d.

**UTILITARIANISM.** By JOHN STUART MILL. New Edition. 8vo. 5s.

**DISSERTATIONS and DISCUSSIONS, POLITICAL, PHILOSOPHI-** CAL, and HISTORICAL. By JOHN STUART MILL. 3 vols. 8vo. 36s.

**EXAMINATION of Sir. W. HAMILTON'S PHILOSOPHY,** and of the Principal Philosophical Questions discussed in his Writings. By JOHN STUART MILL. Fourth Edition. 8vo. 16s.

An **OUTLINE of the NECESSARY LAWS of THOUGHT;** a Treatise on Pure and Applied Logic. By the Most Rev. W. THOMSON, Lord Archbishop of York, D.D. F.R.S. Ninth Thousand. Crown 8vo. price 5s. 6d.

**PRINCIPLES of ECONOMICAL PHILOSOPHY.** By HENRY DUNNING MACLEOD, M.A. Barrister-at-Law. Second Edition. In Two Volumes. VOL. I. 8vo. price 15s.

A **SYSTEM of LOGIC, RATIOCINATIVE and INDUCTIVE.** By JOHN STUART MILL. Eighth Edition. Two vols. 8vo. 25s.

The **ELECTION of REPRESENTATIVES,** Parliamentary and Muni-cipal; a Treatise. By THOMAS HARE, Barrister-at-Law. Crown 8vo. 7s.

**SPEECHES of the RIGHT HON. LORD MACAULAY,** corrected by Himself. People's Edition, crown 8vo. 3s. 6d.

Lord **Macaulay's Speeches** on Parliamentary Reform in 1831 and 1832. 16mo. 1s.

**FAMILIES of SPEECH**: Four Lectures delivered before the Royal Institution of Great Britain. By the Rev. F. W. FARRAR, D.D. F.R.S. New Edition. Crown 8vo. 3s. 6d.

**CHAPTERS on LANGUAGE.** By the Rev. F. W. FARRAR, D.D. F.R.S. New Edition. Crown 8vo. 5s.

A **DICTIONARY of the ENGLISH LANGUAGE.** By R. G. LATHAM, M.A. M.D. F.R.S. Founded on the Dictionary of Dr. SAMUEL JOHNSON, as edited by the Rev. H. J. TODD, with numerous Emendations and Additions. In Four Volumes, 4to. price £7.

A **PRACTICAL ENGLISH DICTIONARY,** on the Plan of White's English-Latin and Latin-English Dictionaries. By JOHN T. WHITE, D.D. Oxon. and T. C. DONKIN, M.A. Assistant-Master, King Edward's Grammar School, Birmingham. Post 8vo. [In the press.

**THESAURUS of ENGLISH WORDS and PHRASES,** classified and arranged so as to facilitate the Expression of Ideas, and assist in Literary Composition. By P. M. ROGET, M.D. New Edition. Crown 8vo. 10s. 6d.

**LECTURES on the SCIENCE of LANGUAGE.** By F. Max Müller, M.A. &c. Seventh Edition. 2 vols. crown 8vo. 16s.

**MANUAL of ENGLISH LITERATURE,** Historical and Critical. By Thomas Arnold, M.A. New Edition. Crown 8vo. 7s. 6d.

**SOUTHEY'S DOCTOR,** complete in One Volume. Edited by the Rev. J. W. Warter, B.D. Square crown 8vo. 12s. 6d.

**HISTORICAL and CRITICAL COMMENTARY on the OLD TESTA-MENT;** with a New Translation. By M. M. Kalisch, Ph.D. Vol. I. *Genesis,* 8vo. 18s. or adapted for the General Reader, 12s. Vol. II. *Exodus,* 15s. or adapted for the General Reader, 12s. Vol. III. *Leviticus,* Part I. 15s. or adapted for the General Reader, 8s. Vol. IV. *Leviticus,* Part II. 15s. or adapted for the General Reader, 8s.

**A DICTIONARY of ROMAN and GREEK ANTIQUITIES,** with about Two Thousand Engravings on Wood from Ancient Originals, illustrative of the Industrial Arts and Social Life of the Greeks and Romans. By A. Rich, B.A. Third Edition, revised and improved. Crown 8vo. price 7s. 6d.

**A LATIN-ENGLISH DICTIONARY.** By John T. White, D.D. Oxon. and J. E. Riddle, M.A. Oxon. Revised Edition. 2 vols. 4to. 42s.

**WHITE'S COLLEGE LATIN-ENGLISH DICTIONARY** (Intermediate Size), abridged for the use of University Students from the Parent Work (as above). Medium 8vo. 15s.

**WHITE'S JUNIOR STUDENT'S COMPLETE LATIN-ENGLISH and ENGLISH-LATIN DICTIONARY.** New Edition. Square 12mo. price 12s.

Separately { The ENGLISH-LATIN DICTIONARY, price 5s. 6d. The LATIN-ENGLISH DICTIONARY, price 7s. 6d.

**A LATIN-ENGLISH DICTIONARY,** adapted for the Use of Middle-Class Schools. By John T. White, D.D. Oxon. Square fcp. 8vo. price 3s.

**An ENGLISH-GREEK LEXICON,** containing all the Greek Words used by Writers of good authority. By C. D. Yonge, B.A. New Edition. 4to. price 21s.

**Mr. YONGE'S NEW LEXICON, English and Greek,** abridged from his larger work (as above). Revised Edition. Square 12mo. price 8s. 6d.

**A GREEK-ENGLISH LEXICON.** Compiled by H. G. Liddell, D.D. Dean of Christ Church, and R. Scott, D.D. Dean of Rochester. Sixth Edition. Crown 4to. price 36s.

**A Lexicon, Greek and English,** abridged from Liddell and Scott's *Greek-English Lexicon.* Fourteenth Edition. Square 12mo. 7s. 6d.

**A SANSKRIT-ENGLISH DICTIONARY,** the Sanskrit words printed both in the original Devanagari and in Roman Letters. Compiled by T. Benfey, Prof. in the Univ. of Göttingen. 8vo. 52s. 6d.

**A PRACTICAL DICTIONARY of the FRENCH and ENGLISH LAN-GUAGES.** By L. Contanseau. Revised Edition. Post 8vo. 10s. 6d.

**Contanseau's Pocket Dictionary,** French and English, abridged from the above by the Author. New Edition, revised. Square 18mo. 5s. 6d.

**NEW PRACTICAL DICTIONARY of the GERMAN LANGUAGE;** German-English and English-German. By the Rev. W. L. Blackley, M.A. and Dr. Carl Martin Friedländer. Post 8vo. 7s. 6d.

The MASTERY of LANGUAGES; or, the Art of Speaking Foreign Tongues Idiomatically. By THOMAS PRENDERGAST. 8vo. 6s.

## Miscellaneous Works and Popular Metaphysics.

ESSAYS on FREETHINKING and PLAIN-SPEAKING. By LESLIE STEPHEN. Crown 8vo. 10s. 6d.

THE MISCELLANEOUS WORKS of THOMAS ARNOLD, D.D. Late Head Master of Rugby School and Regius Professor of Modern History in the University of Oxford, collected and republished. 8vo. 7s. 6d.

MISCELLANEOUS and POSTHUMOUS WORKS of the Late HENRY THOMAS BUCKLE. Edited, with a Biographical Notice, by HELEN TAYLOR. 3 vols. 8vo. price 52s. 6d.

MISCELLANEOUS WRITINGS of JOHN CONINGTON, M.A. late Corpus Professor of Latin in the University of Oxford. Edited by J. A. SYMONDS, M.A. With a Memoir by H. J. S. SMITH, M.A. 2 vols. 8vo. 28s.

ESSAYS, CRITICAL and BIOGRAPHICAL. Contributed to the *Edinburgh Review*. By HENRY ROGERS. New Edition, with Additions. 2 vols. crown 8vo. price 12s.

ESSAYS on some THEOLOGICAL CONTROVERSIES of the TIME. Contributed chiefly to the *Edinburgh Review*. By HENRY ROGERS. New Edition, with Additions. Crown 8vo. price 6s.

LANDSCAPES, CHURCHES, and MORALITIES. By A. K. H. B. Crown 8vo. price 3s. 6d.

Recreations of a Country Parson. By A. K. H. B. FIRST and SECOND SERIES, crown 8vo. 3s. 6d. each.

The Common-place Philosopher in Town and Country. By A. K. H. B. Crown 8vo. price 3s. 6d.

Leisure Hours in Town; Essays Consolatory, Æsthetical, Moral, Social, and Domestic. By A. K. H. B. Crown 8vo. 3s. 6d.

The Autumn Holidays of a Country Parson; Essays contributed to *Fraser's Magazine*, &c. By A. K. H. B. Crown 8vo. 3s. 6d.

Seaside Musings on Sundays and Week-Days. By A. K. H. B. Crown 8vo. price 3s. 6d.

The Graver Thoughts of a Country Parson. By A. K. H. B. FIRST and SECOND SERIES, crown 8vo. 3s. 6d. each.

Critical Essays of a Country Parson, selected from Essays contributed to *Fraser's Magazine*. By A. K. H. B. Crown 8vo. 3s. 6d.

Sunday Afternoons at the Parish Church of a Scottish University City. By A. K. H. B. Crown 8vo. 3s. 6d.

Lessons of Middle Age; with some Account of various Cities and Men. By A. K. H. B. Crown 8vo. 3s. 6d.

Counsel and Comfort spoken from a City Pulpit. By A. K. H. B. Crown 8vo. price 3s. 6d.

**CHANGED ASPECTS of UNCHANGED TRUTHS; Memorials of St.**
Andrews Sundays. By A. K. H. B. Crown 8vo. 3s. 6d.

**Present-day Thoughts; Memorials of St. Andrews Sundays.** By
A. K. H. B. Crown 8vo. 3s. 6d.

**SHORT STUDIES on GREAT SUBJECTS.** By JAMES ANTHONY
FROUDE, M.A. late Fellow of Exeter Coll. Oxford. 2 vols. crown 8vo. price 12s.

**LORD MACAULAY'S MISCELLANEOUS WRITINGS:—**

> LIBRARY EDITION. 2 vols. 8vo. Portrait, 21s.
> PEOPLE'S EDITION. 1 vol. crown 8vo. 4s. 6d.

**LORD MACAULAY'S MISCELLANEOUS WRITINGS and SPEECHES.**

> STUDENT'S EDITION, in crown 8vo. price 6s.

**The Rev. SYDNEY SMITH'S ESSAYS** contributed to the Edinburgh
Review. Authorised Edition, complete in 1 vol. Crown 8vo. price 2s. 6d.

**The Rev. SYDNEY SMITH'S MISCELLANEOUS WORKS;** including
his Contributions to the *Edinburgh Review*. Crown 8vo. 6s.

**The Wit and Wisdom of the Rev. Sydney Smith;** a Selection of
the most memorable Passages in his Writings and Conversation. 16mo. 3s. 6d.

**The ECLIPSE of FAITH;** or, a Visit to a Religious Sceptic. By
HENRY ROGERS. Latest Edition. Fcp. 8vo. price 5s.

**Defence of the Eclipse of Faith, by its Author;** a rejoinder to Dr.
Newman's *Reply*. Latest Edition. Fcp 8vo. price 3s. 6d.

**CHIPS from a GERMAN WORKSHOP;** Essays on the Science of
Religion, and on Mythology, Traditions, and Customs. By F. MAX MÜLLER,
M.A. &c. Second Edition. 3 vols. 8vo. £2.

**ANALYSIS of the PHENOMENA of the HUMAN MIND.** By
JAMES MILL. A New Edition, with Notes, Illustrative and Critical, by
ALEXANDER BAIN, ANDREW FINDLATER, and GEORGE GROTE. Edited, with
additional Notes, by JOHN STUART MILL. 2 vols. 8vo. price 28s.

**An INTRODUCTION to MENTAL PHILOSOPHY, on the Inductive**
Method. By J. D. MORELL, M.A. LL.D. 8vo. 12s.

**ELEMENTS of PSYCHOLOGY,** containing the Analysis of the
Intellectual Powers. By J. D. MORELL, M.A. LL.D. Post 8vo. 7s. 6d.

**The SECRET of HEGEL;** being the Hegelian System in Origin,
Principle, Form, and Matter. By J. H. STIRLING, LL.D. 2 vols. 8vo. 28s.

**SIR WILLIAM HAMILTON;** being the Philosophy of Perception: an
Analysis. By J. H. STIRLING, LL.D. 8vo. 5s.

**The SENSES and the INTELLECT.** By ALEXANDER BAIN, M.D.
Professor of Logic in the University of Aberdeen. Third Edition. 8vo. 15s.

**MENTAL and MORAL SCIENCE:** a Compendium of Psychology
and Ethics. By the same Author. Third Edition. Crown 8vo. 10s. 6d. Or
separately: PART I. *Mental Science*, 6s. 6d. PART II. *Moral Science*, 4s. 6d.

**LOGIC, DEDUCTIVE and INDUCTIVE.** By the same Author. In
Two Parts, crown 8vo. 10s. 6d. Each Part may be had separately:—
PART I. *Deduction*, 4s. PART II. *Induction*, 6s. 6d.

The PHILOSOPHY of NECESSITY; or, Natural Law as applicable to Mental, Moral, and Social Science. By CHARLES BRAY. 8vo. 9s.

On FORCE, its MENTAL and MORAL CORRELATES. By the same Author. 8vo. 5s.

A MANUAL of ANTHROPOLOGY, or SCIENCE of MAN, based on Modern Research. By CHARLES BRAY. Crown 8vo. price 6s.

A PHRENOLOGIST AMONGST the TODAS, or the Study of a Primitive Tribe in South India; History, Character, Customs, Religion, Infanticide, Polyandry, Language. By W. E. MARSHALL, Lieutenant-Colonel B.S.C. With 26 Illustrations. 8vo 21s.

A TREATISE of HUMAN NATURE, being an Attempt to Introduce the Experimental Method of Reasoning into Moral Subjects; followed by Dialogues concerning Natural Religion. By DAVID HUME. Edited, with Notes, &c. by T. H. GREEN, Fellow and Tutor, Ball. Coll. and T. H. GROSE, Fellow and Tutor, Queen's Coll. Oxford. 2 vols. 8vo. 28s.

ESSAYS MORAL, POLITICAL, and LITERARY. By DAVID HUME. By the same Editors. 2 vols. 8vo. price 28s.

UEBERWEG'S SYSTEM of LOGIC and HISTORY of LOGICAL DOCTRINES. Translated, with Notes and Appendices, by T. M. LINDSAY, M.A. F.R.S.E. 8vo. price 16s.

A BUDGET of PARADOXES. By AUGUSTUS DE MORGAN, F.R.A.S. and C.P.S. 8vo. 15s.

## Astronomy, Meteorology, Popular Geography, &c.

BRINKLEY'S ASTRONOMY. Revised and partly re-written, with Additional Chapters, and an Appendix of Questions for Examination. By J. W. STUBBS, D.D. Fellow and Tutor of Trinity College, Dublin, and F. BRUNNOW, Ph.D. Astronomer Royal of Ireland. Crown 8vo. price 6s.

OUTLINES of ASTRONOMY. By Sir J. F. W. HERSCHEL, Bart. M.A. Latest Edition, with Plates and Diagrams. Square crown 8vo. 12s.

ESSAYS on ASTRONOMY, a Series of Papers on Planets and Meteors, the Sun and Sun-surrounding Space, Stars and Star-Cloudlets; with a Dissertation on the approaching Transit of Venus. By RICHARD A. PROCTOR, B.A. With 10 Plates and 24 Woodcuts. 8vo. 12s.

THE TRANSITS of VENUS; a Popular Account of Past and Coming Transits, from the first observed by Horrocks A.D. 1639 to the Transit of A.D. 2112. By R. A. PROCTOR, B.A. Cantab. With 20 Plates and numerous Woodcuts. Crown 8vo. [Nearly ready.

The UNIVERSE and the COMING TRANSITS: Presenting Researches into and New Views respecting the Constitution of the Heavens; together with an Investigation of the Conditions of the Coming Transits of Venus. By R. A. PROCTOR, B.A. With 22 Charts and 22 Woodcuts. 8vo. 16s.

The MOON; her Motions, Aspect, Scenery, and Physical Condition. By R. A. PROCTOR, B.A. With Plates, Charts, Woodcuts, and Three Lunar Photographs. Crown 8vo. 15s.

The SUN; RULER, LIGHT, FIRE, and LIFE of the PLANETARY SYSTEM. By R. A. PROCTOR, B.A. Second Edition, with 10 Plates (7 coloured) and 107 Figures on Wood. Crown 8vo. 14s.

OTHER WORLDS THAN OURS; the Plurality of Worlds Studied under the Light of Recent Scientific Researches. By R. A. PROCTOR, B.A. Third Edition, with 14 Illustrations. Crown 8vo. 10s. 6d.

The ORBS AROUND US; a Series of Familiar Essays on the Moon and Planets, Meteors and Comets, the Sun and Coloured Pairs of Stars. By R. A. PROCTOR, B.A. Crown 8vo. price 7s. 6d.

SATURN and its SYSTEM. By R. A. PROCTOR, B.A. 8vo. with 14 Plates, 14s.

SCHELLEN'S SPECTRUM ANALYSIS, in its application to Terrestrial Substances and the Physical Constitution of the Heavenly Bodies. Translated by JANE and C. LASSELL; edited, with Notes, by W. HUGGINS, LL.D. F.R.S. With 13 Plates (6 coloured) and 225 Woodcuts. 8vo. price 28s.

A NEW STAR ATLAS, for the Library, the School, and the Observatory, in Twelve Circular Maps (with Two Index Plates). Intended as a Companion to 'Webb's Celestial Objects for Common Telescopes.' With a Letterpress Introduction on the Study of the Stars, Illustrated by 9 Diagrams. By R. A. PROCTOR, B.A. Crown 8vo. 5s.

CELESTIAL OBJECTS for COMMON TELESCOPES. By the Rev. T. W. WEBB, M.A. F.R.A.S. Third Edition, revised and enlarged; with Maps, Plate, and Woodcuts. Crown 8vo. price 7s. 6d.

AIR and RAIN; the Beginnings of a Chemical Climatology. By ROBERT ANGUS SMITH, Ph.D. F.R.S. F.C.S. With 8 Illustrations. 8vo. 24s.

NAUTICAL SURVEYING, an INTRODUCTION to the PRACTICAL and THEORETICAL STUDY of. By J. K. LAUGHTON, M.A. Small 8vo. 6s.

MAGNETISM and DEVIATION of the COMPASS. For the Use of Students in Navigation and Science Schools. By J. MERRIFIELD, LL.D. 18mo. 1s. 6d.

DOVE'S LAW of STORMS, considered in connexion with the Ordinary Movements of the Atmosphere. Translated by R. H. SCOTT, M.A. 8vo. 10s. 6d.

KEITH JOHNSTON'S GENERAL DICTIONARY of GEOGRAPHY, Descriptive, Physical, Statistical, and Historical; forming a complete Gazetteer of the World. New Edition, revised and corrected to the Present Date by the Author's Son, KEITH JOHNSTON, F.R.G.S. 1 vol. 8vo.          [Nearly ready.

The POST OFFICE GAZETTEER of the UNITED KINGDOM. Being a Complete Dictionary of all Cities, Towns, Villages, and of the Principal Gentlemen's Seats, in Great Britain and Ireland; Referred to the nearest Post Town, Railway and Telegraph Station: with Natural Features and Objects of Note. By J. A. SHARP. 1 vol. 8vo. of about 1,500 pages.          [In the press.

The PUBLIC SCHOOLS ATLAS of MODERN GEOGRAPHY. In 31 Maps, exhibiting clearly the more important Physical Features of the Countries delineated, and Noting all the Chief Places of Historical, Commercial, or Social Interest. Edited, with an Introduction, by the Rev. G. BUTLER, M.A. Imp. 4to. price 8s. 6d. sewed, or 5s. cloth.

The PUBLIC SCHOOLS MANUAL of MODERN GEOGRAPHY. By the Rev. GEORGE BUTLER, M.A. Principal of Liverpool College; Editor of 'The Public Schools Atlas of Modern Geography.'          [In preparation.

The **PUBLIC SCHOOLS ATLAS** of **ANCIENT GEOGRAPHY** Edited,
with an Introduction on the Study of Ancient Geography, by the Rev. GEORGE
BUTLER, M.A. Principal of Liverpool College. Imperial Quarto.
[*In preparation.*

A **MANUAL** of **GEOGRAPHY**, Physical, Industrial, and Political.
By W. HUGHES, F.R.G.S. With 6 Maps. Fcp. 7s. 6d.

**MAUNDER'S TREASURY** of **GEOGRAPHY**, Physical, Historical,
Descriptive, and Political. Edited by W. HUGHES, F.R.G.S. Revised Edition,
with 7 Maps and 16 Plates. Fcp. 6s. cloth, or 10s. bound in calf.

## *Natural History* and *Popular Science.*

**TEXT-BOOKS** of **SCIENCE, MECHANICAL** and **PHYSICAL,**
adapted for the use of Artisans and of Students in Public and Science Schools.
Edited by T. M. GOODEVE, M.A. and C. W. MERRIFIELD, F.R.S.

ANDERSON's Strength of Materials, small 8vo. 3s. 6d.
ARMSTRONG's Organic Chemistry, 3s. 6d.
BLOXAM's Metals, 3s. 6d.
GOODEVE's Elements of Mechanism, 3s. 6d.
———— Principles of Mechanics, 3s. 6d.
GRIFFIN's Algebra and Trigonometry, 3s. 6d. Notes, 3s.6d.
JENKIN's Electricity and Magnetism, 3s. 6d.
MAXWELL's Theory of Heat, 3s. 6d.
MERRIFIELD's Technical Arithmetic and Mensuration, 3s. 6d. Key, 3s. 6d.
MILLER's Inorganic Chemistry, 3s. 6d.
SHELLEY's Workshop Appliances, 3s. 6d.
THORPE's Quantitative Chemical Analysis, 4s. 6d.
THORPE & MUIR's Qualitative Analysis, 3s. 6d.
WATSON's Plane and Solid Geometry, 3s. 6d.

*₊* Other Text-Books in active preparation.

**ELEMENTARY TREATISE** on **PHYSICS,** Experimental and Applied.
Translated and edited from GANOT's *Éléments de Physique* by E. ATKINSON,
Ph.D. F.C.S. New Edition, revised and enlarged; with a Coloured Plate and
720 Woodcuts. Post 8vo. 15s.

**NATURAL PHILOSOPHY** for **GENERAL READERS** and **YOUNG**
PERSONS; being a Course of Physics divested of Mathematical Formulæ
expressed in the language of daily life. Translated from GANOT's *Cours de
Physique* and by E. ATKINSON, Ph.D. F.C.S. Crown 8vo. with 404 Woodcuts,
price 7s. 6d.

**HELMHOLTZ'S POPULAR LECTURES** on **SCIENTIFIC SUBJECTS.**
Translated by E. ATKINSON, Ph.D. F.C.S. Professor of Experimental Science,
Staff College. With an Introduction by Professor TYNDALL. 8vo. with nume-
rous Woodcuts, price 12s. 6d.

**SOUND:** a Course of Eight Lectures delivered at the Royal Institution
of Great Britain. By JOHN TYNDALL, LL.D. D.C.L. F.R.S. New Edition,
with 169 Woodcuts. Crown 8vo. 9s.

**HEAT a MODE of MOTION.** By JOHN TYNDALL, LL.D. D.C.L
F.R.S. Fourth Edition. Crown 8vo. with Woodcuts, 10s. 6d.

**CONTRIBUTIONS to MOLECULAR PHYSICS in the DOMAIN of**
RADIANT HEAT. By J. Tyndall, LL.D. D.C.L. F.R.S. With 2 Plates and
31 Woodcuts. 8vo. 16s.

**RESEARCHES on DIAMAGNETISM and MAGNE-CRYSTALLIC**
ACTION; including the Question of Diamagnetic Polarity. By J. Tyndall,
M.D. D.C.L. F.R.S. With 6 plates and many Woodcuts. 8vo. 14s.

**NOTES of a COURSE of SEVEN LECTURES on ELECTRICAL**
PHENOMENA and THEORIES, delivered at the Royal Institution, A.D. 1870.
By John Tyndall, LL.D., D.C.L., F.R.S. Crown 8vo. 1s. sewed; 1s. 6d. cloth.

**A TREATISE on MAGNETISM,** General and Terrestrial. By Humphrey Lloyd, D.D., D.C.L., Provost of Trinity College, Dublin. 8vo. price
10s. 6d.

**ELEMENTARY TREATISE on the WAVE-THEORY of LIGHT.**
By Humphrey Lloyd, D.D. D.C.L. Provost of Trinity College, Dublin. Third
Edition, revised and enlarged. 8vo. price 10s. 6d.

**LECTURES on LIGHT** delivered in the United States of America in
the Years 1872 and 1873. By John Tyndall, LL.D. D.C.L. F.R.S. With
Frontispiece and Diagrams. Crown 8vo. price 7s. 6d.

**NOTES of a COURSE of NINE LECTURES on LIGHT** delivered at the
Royal Institution, A.D. 1869. By John Tyndall, LL.D. D.C.L. F.R.S.
Crown 8vo. price 1s. sewed, or 1s. 6d. cloth.

**ADDRESS** delivered before the British Association assembled at
Belfast; with Additions and a Preface. By John Tyndall, F.R.S. President.
8vo. price 3s.

**FRAGMENTS of SCIENCE.** By John Tyndall, LL.D. D.C.L. F.R.S.
Third Edition. 8vo. price 14s.

**LIGHT SCIENCE for LEISURE HOURS;** a Series of Familiar
Essays on Scientific Subjects, Natural Phenomena, &c. By R. A. Proctor,
B.A. First and Second Series. Crown 8vo. 7s. 6d. each.

**The CORRELATION of PHYSICAL FORCES.** By the Hon. Sir W. R.
Grove, M.A. F.R.S. one of the Judges of the Court of Common Pleas. Sixth
Edition, with other Contributions to Science. 8vo. price 15s.

**Professor OWEN'S LECTURES on the COMPARATIVE ANATOMY**
and Physiology of the Invertebrate Animals. Second Edition, with 235 Woodcuts.
8vo. 21s.

**The COMPARATIVE ANATOMY and PHYSIOLOGY of the VERTE-**
BRATE ANIMALS. By Richard Owen, F.R.S. D.C.L. With 1,472 Woodcuts.
3 vols. 8vo. £3. 13s. 6d.

**PRINCIPLES of ANIMAL MECHANICS.** By the Rev. S. Haughton,
F.R.S. Fellow of Trin. Coll. Dubl. M.D. Dubl. and D.C.L. Oxon. Second
Edition, with 111 Figures on Wood. 8vo. 21s.

**ROCKS CLASSIFIED and DESCRIBED.** By Bernhard Von Cotta.
English Edition, by P. H. Lawrence; with English, German, and French
Synonymes. Post 8vo. 14s.

**The ANCIENT STONE IMPLEMENTS, WEAPONS, and ORNA-**
MENTS of GREAT BRITAIN. By John Evans, F.R.S. F.S.A. With 2 Plates
and 476 Woodcuts. 8vo. price 28s.

**PRIMEVAL WORLD of SWITZERLAND.** By Professor OSWALD HEER, of the University of Zurich. Translated by W. S. DALLAS, F.L.S., and edited by JAMES HEYWOOD, M.A., F.R.S. 2 vols. 8vo. with numerous Illustrations. [*In the press.*]

**The ORIGIN of CIVILISATION and the PRIMITIVE CONDITION** of MAN ; Mental and Social Condition of Savages. By Sir JOHN LUBBOCK, Bart. M.P. F.R.S. Third Edition, revised, with Woodcuts. [*Nearly ready.*]

**BIBLE ANIMALS;** being a Description of every Living Creature mentioned in the Scriptures, from the Ape to the Coral. By the Rev. J. G. WOOD, M.A. F.L.S. With about 100 Vignettes on Wood. 8vo. 21s.

**HOMES WITHOUT HANDS;** a Description of the Habitations of Animals, classed according to their Principle of Construction. By the Rev. J. G. WOOD, M.A. F.L.S. With about 140 Vignettes on Wood. 8vo. 21s.

**INSECTS AT HOME;** a Popular Account of British Insects, their Structure, Habits, and Transformations. By the Rev. J. G. WOOD, M.A. F.L.S. With upwards of 700 Illustrations. 8vo. price 21s.

**INSECTS ABROAD;** a Popular Account of Foreign Insects, their Structure, Habits, and Transformations. By J. G. WOOD, M.A. F.L.S. Printed and Illustrated uniformly with 'Insects at Home.' 8vo. price 21s.

**STRANGE DWELLINGS;** a description of the Habitations of Animals, abridged from 'Homes without Hands.' By the Rev. J. G. WOOD, M.A. F.L.S. With about 60 Woodcut Illustrations. Crown 8vo. price 7s. 6d.

**OUT of DOORS;** a Selection of original Articles on Practical Natural History. By the Rev. J. G. WOOD, M.A. F.L.S. With Eleven Illustrations from Original Designs engraved on Wood by G. Pearson. Crown 8vo. price 7s. 6d.

**A FAMILIAR HISTORY of BIRDS.** By E. STANLEY, D.D. F.R.S. late Lord Bishop of Norwich. Seventh Edition, with Woodcuts. Fcp. 3s. 6d.

**FROM JANUARY to DECEMBER;** a Book for Children. Second Edition. 8vo. 3s. 6d.

**The SEA and its LIVING WONDERS.** By Dr. GEORGE HARTWIG. Latest revised Edition. 8vo. with many Illustrations, 10s. 6d.

**The TROPICAL WORLD.** By Dr. GEORGE HARTWIG. With above 160 Illustrations. Latest revised Edition. 8vo. price 10s. 6d.

**The SUBTERRANEAN WORLD.** By Dr. GEORGE HARTWIG. With 3 Maps and about 80 Woodcuts, including 8 full size of page. 8vo. price 21s.

**THE AERIAL WORLD.** By Dr. GEORGE HARTWIG. With 8 Chromoxylographs and 60 Illustrations engraved on Wood. 8vo. price 21s.

**The POLAR WORLD,** a Popular Description of Man and Nature in the Arctic and Antarctic Regions of the Globe. By Dr. GEORGE HARTWIG. With 8 Chromoxylographs, 3 Maps, and 85 Woodcuts. 8vo. 10s. 6d.

**KIRBY and SPENCE'S INTRODUCTION to ENTOMOLOGY,** or Elements of the Natural History of Insects. 7th Edition. Crown 8vo. 5s.

**MAUNDER'S TREASURY of NATURAL HISTORY,** or Popular Dictionary of Birds, Beasts, Fishes, Reptiles, Insects, and Creeping Things. With above 900 Woodcuts. Fcp. 8vo. price 6s. cloth, or 10s. bound in calf.

**MAUNDER'S SCIENTIFIC and LITERARY TREASURY.** New Edition, thoroughly revised and in great part rewritten, with above 1,000 new Articles, by J. Y. JOHNSON. Fcp. 8vo. 6s. cloth, or 10s. calf.

**HANDBOOK of HARDY TREES, SHRUBS, and HERBACEOUS**
PLANTS, containing Descriptions, Native Countries, &c. of a Selection of the
Best Species in Cultivation; together with Cultural Details, Comparative
Hardiness, Suitability for Particular Positions, &c. By W. B. HEMSLEY. Based on
DECAISNE and NAUDIN's *Manuel de l'Amateur des Jardins*, and including the 264
Original Woodcuts. Medium 8vo. 21*s.*

**A GENERAL SYSTEM of BOTANY DESCRIPTIVE and ANALYTICAL.**
I. Outlines of Organography, Anatomy, and Physiology; II. Descriptions and
Illustrations of the Orders. By E. LE MAOUT, and J. DECAISNE, Members of
the Institute of France. Translated by Mrs. HOOKER. The Orders arranged
after the Method followed in the Universities and Schools of Great Britain, its
Colonies, America, and India; with an Appendix on the Natural Method, and
other Additions, by J. D. HOOKER, F.R.S. &c. Director of the Royal Botanical
Gardens, Kew. With 5,500 Woodcuts. Imperial 8vo. price 52*s.* 6*d.*

**The TREASURY of BOTANY, or Popular Dictionary of the Vegetable**
Kingdom; including a Glossary of Botanical Terms. Edited by J. LINDLEY,
F.R.S. and T. MOORE, F.L.S. assisted by eminent Contributors. With 274
Woodcuts and 20 Steel Plates. Two Parts, fcp. 8vo. 12*s.* cloth, or 20*s.* calf.

**The ELEMENTS of BOTANY for FAMILIES and SCHOOLS.**
Tenth Edition, revised by THOMAS MOORE, F.L.S. Fcp. with 154 Woodcuts, 2*s.* 6*d.*

**The ROSE AMATEUR'S GUIDE.** By THOMAS RIVERS. Fourteenth
Edition. Fcp. 8vo. 4*s.*

**LOUDON'S ENCYCLOPÆDIA of PLANTS**; comprising the Specific
Character, Description, Culture, History, &c. of all the Plants found in
Great Britain. With upwards of 12,000 Woodcuts. 8vo. 42*s.*

**A DICTIONARY of SCIENCE, LITERATURE, and ART.** Fourth
Edition, re-edited by W. T. BRANDE (the original Author), and GEORGE W.
COX, M.A., assisted by contributors of eminent Scientific and Literary
Acquirements. 3 vols. medium 8vo. price 63*s.* cloth.

---

## Chemistry and Physiology.

**A DICTIONARY of CHEMISTRY** and the Allied Branches of other
Sciences. By HENRY WATTS, F.R.S. assisted by eminent Contributors.
5 vols. medium 8vo. price £8. 14*s.* 6*d.* SECOND SUPPLEMENT *in the Press.*

**ELEMENTS of CHEMISTRY,** Theoretical and Practical. By W. ALLEN
MILLER, M.D. late Prof. of Chemistry, King's Coll. London. New
Edition. 3 vols. 8vo. £3. PART I. CHEMICAL PHYSICS, 15*s.* PART II.
INORGANIC CHEMISTRY, 21*s.* PART III. ORGANIC CHEMISTRY, 24*s.*

**A Course of Practical Chemistry,** for the use of Medical Students.
By W. ODLING, F.R.S. New Edition, with 70 Woodcuts. Crown 8vo. 7*s.* 6*d.*

**A MANUAL of CHEMICAL PHYSIOLOGY,** including its Points of
Contact with Pathology. By J. L. W. THUDICHUM, M.D. With Woodcuts.
8vo. price 7*s.* 6*d.*

**SELECT METHODS in CHEMICAL ANALYSIS,** chiefly INOR-
GANIC. By WILLIAM CROOKES, F.R.S. With 22 Woodcuts. Crown 8vo.
price 12*s.* 6*d.*

**A PRACTICAL HANDBOOK of DYEING and CALICO PRINTING.**
By WILLIAM CROOKES, F.R.S. With 11 Page Plates, 49 Specimens of Dyed and
Printed Fabrics, and 36 Woodcuts.  8vo. 42s.

**OUTLINES of PHYSIOLOGY, Human and Comparative.** By JOHN
MARSHALL, F.R.C.S. Surgeon to the University College Hospital.  2 vols.
crown 8vo. with 122 Woodcuts, 32s.

**PHYSIOLOGICAL ANATOMY and PHYSIOLOGY of MAN.** By the
late R. B. TODD, M.D. F.R.S. and W. BOWMAN, F.R.S. of King's College.
With numerous Illustrations.  Vol. II. 8vo. 25s.

VOL. I. New Edition by Dr. LIONEL S. BEALE, F.R.S. in course of publication, with many Illustrations.  PARTS I. and II. price 7s. 6d. each.

---

## The Fine Arts, and Illustrated Editions.

**A DICTIONARY of ARTISTS of the ENGLISH SCHOOL:** Painters,
Sculptors, Architects, Engravers, and Ornamentists; with Notices of their Lives
and Works.  By S. REDGRAVE.  8vo. 16s.

**The THREE CATHEDRALS DEDICATED to ST. PAUL, in LONDON;**
their History from the Foundation of the First Building in the Sixth Century
to the Proposals for the Adornment of the Present Cathedral.  By WILLIAM
LONGMAN, F.A.S.  With numerous Illustrations.  Square crown 8vo. 21s.

**IN FAIRYLAND;** Pictures from the Elf-World.  By RICHARD
DOYLE.  With a Poem by W. ALLINGHAM.  With Sixteen Plates, containing
Thirty-six Designs printed in Colours.  Second Edition.  Folio, price 15s.

**ALBERT DURER, HIS LIFE and WORKS;** including Auto-
biographical Papers and Complete Catalogues.  By WILLIAM B. SCOTT.
With Six Etchings by the Author, and other Illustrations.  8vo. 16s.

**The NEW TESTAMENT,** illustrated with Wood Engravings after the
Early Masters, chiefly of the Italian School.  Crown 4to. 63s. cloth, gilt top;
or £5 5s. elegantly bound in morocco.

**LYRA GERMANICA;** the Christian Year and the Christian Life.
Translated by CATHERINE WINKWORTH.  With about 325 Woodcut Illustrations
by J. LEIGHTON, F.S.A. and other Artists.  2 vols. 4to. price 42s.

**The LIFE of MAN SYMBOLISED by the MONTHS of the YEAR.**
Text selected by R. PIGOT; Illustrations on Wood from Original Designs
J. LEIGHTON, F.S.A.  4to. 42s.

**SACRED and LEGENDARY ART.** By MRS. JAMESON.

**Legends of the Saints and Martyrs.**  New Edition, with 19
Etchings and 187 Woodcuts.  2 vols. square crown 8vo. 31s. 6d.

**Legends of the Monastic Orders.**  New Edition, with 11 Etchings
and 88 Woodcuts.  1 vol. square crown 8vo. 21s.

**Legends of the Madonna.**  New Edition, with 27 Etchings and
165 Woodcuts.  1 vol. square crown 8vo. 21s.

**The History of Our Lord,** with that of his Types and Precursors.
Completed by Lady EASTLAKE.  Revised Edition, with 31 Etchings and
281 Woodcuts.  2 vols. square crown 8vo. 42s.

B

**DAEDALUS**; or, the Causes and Principles of the Excellence of Greek Sculpture. By EDWARD FALKENER, Member of the Academy of Bologna, and of the Archæological Institutes of Rome and Berlin. With Woodcuts, Photographs, and Chromolithographs. Royal 8vo. 42s. ;

**FALKENER'S MUSEUM of CLASSICAL ANTIQUITIES**; a Series of Essays on Ancient Art. New Edition, complete in One Volume, with many Illustrations. Royal 8vo. price 12s.

---

## The Useful Arts, Manufactures, &c.

**HISTORY of the GOTHIC REVIVAL**; an Attempt to shew how far the taste for Medieval Architecture was retained in England during the last two centuries, and has been re-developed in the present. By C. L. EAST-LAKE, Architect. With 48 Illustrations. Imperial 8vo. 31s. 6d.

**GWILT'S ENCYCLOPÆDIA of ARCHITECTURE**, with above 1,600 Engravings on Wood. Fifth Edition, revised and enlarged by WYATT PAPWORTH. 8vo. 52s. 6d.

**A MANUAL of ARCHITECTURE**: being a Concise History and Explanation of the principal Styles of European Architecture, Ancient, Medieval, and Renaissance; with a Glossary of Technical Terms. By THOMAS MITCHELL. Crown 8vo. with 150 Woodcuts, 10s. 6d.

**HINTS on HOUSEHOLD TASTE in FURNITURE, UPHOLSTERY**, and other Details. By CHARLES L. EASTLAKE, Architect. New Edition, with about 90 Illustrations. Square crown 8vo. 14s.

**PRINCIPLES of MECHANISM**, designed for the Use of Students in the Universities, and for Engineering Students generally. By R. WILLIS, M.A. F.R.S. &c. Jacksonian Professor in the University of Cambridge. Second Edition, enlarged; with 374 Woodcuts. 8vo. 18s.

**GEOMETRIC TURNING**; comprising a Description of Plant's New Geometric Chuck, with directions for its use, and a series of Patterns cut by it, with Explanations. By H. S. SAVORY. With numerous Woodcuts. 8vo. 21s.

**LATHES and TURNING, Simple, Mechanical, and Ornamental.** By W. HENRY NORTHCOTT. With about 240 Illustrations. 8vo. 18s.

**PERSPECTIVE**; or, the Art of Drawing what One Sees. Explained and adapted to the use of those Sketching from Nature. By Lieut. W. H. COLLINS, R.E. F.R.A.S. With 37 Woodcuts. Crown 8vo. price 5s.

**INDUSTRIAL CHEMISTRY**; a Manual for Manufacturers and for use in Colleges or Technical Schools. Being a Translation of Professors Stohmann and Engler's German Edition of PAYEN'S *Précis de Chimie Industrielle*, by Dr. J. D. BARRY. Edited and supplemented by B. H. PAUL, Ph.D. 8vo. with Plates and Woodcuts. [In the press.

**URE'S DICTIONARY of ARTS, MANUFACTURES, and MINES.** Sixth Edition, rewritten and enlarged by ROBERT HUNT, F.R.S. assisted by numerous Contributors eminent in Science and the Arts, and familiar with Manufactures. With above 2,000 Woodcuts. 3 vols. medium 8vo. £4 14s. 6d.

**HANDBOOK of PRACTICAL TELEGRAPHY.** By R. S. Culley, Memb. Inst. C.E. Engineer-in-Chief of Telegraphs to the Post Office. Sixth Edition, with 144 Woodcuts and 5 Plates. 8vo. price 16s.

**The ENGINEER'S HANDBOOK;** explaining the Principles which should guide the Young Engineer in the Construction of Machinery, with the necessary Rules, Proportions, and Tables. By C. S. Lowndes. Post 8vo. 5s.

**ENCYCLOPÆDIA of CIVIL ENGINEERING,** Historical, Theoretical, and Practical. By E. Cresy, C.E. With above 3,000 Woodcuts. 8vo. 42s.

**The STRAINS IN TRUSSES** computed by means of Diagrams; with 20 Examples drawn to Scale. By F. A. Ranken, M.A. C.E. With 35 Diagrams. Square crown 8vo. 6s. 6d.

**TREATISE on MILLS and MILLWORK.** By Sir W. Fairbairn, Bart. F.R.S. New Edition, with 18 Plates and 333 Woodcuts, 2 vols. 8vo. 32s.

**USEFUL INFORMATION for ENGINEERS.** By Sir W. Fairbairn, Bart. F.R.S. Revised Edition, with Illustrations. 3 vols. crown 8vo. price 31s. 6d.

**The APPLICATION of CAST and WROUGHT IRON to Building** Purposes. By Sir W. Fairbairn, Bart. F.R.S. Fourth Edition, enlarged; with 6 Plates and 118 Woodcuts. 8vo. price 16s.

**GUNS and STEEL;** Miscellaneous Papers on Mechanical Subjects. By Sir Joseph Whitworth, Bart. C.E. Royal 8vo. with Illustrations, 7s. 6d.

**A TREATISE on the STEAM ENGINE,** in its various Applications to Mines, Mills, Steam Navigation, Railways, and Agriculture. By J. Bourne, C.E. Eighth Edition; with Portrait, 37 Plates, and 546 Woodcuts. 4to. 42s.

**CATECHISM of the STEAM ENGINE,** in its various Applications to Mines, Mills, Steam Navigation, Railways, and Agriculture. By the same Author. With 89 Woodcuts. Fcp. 8vo. 6s.

**HANDBOOK of the STEAM ENGINE.** By the same Author, forming a Key to the Catechism of the Steam Engine, with 67 Woodcuts. Fcp. 9s.

**BOURNE'S RECENT IMPROVEMENTS in the STEAM ENGINE** in its various applications to Mines, Mills, Steam Navigation, Railways, and Agriculture. By John Bourne, C.E. New Edition, with 124 Woodcuts. Fcp. 8vo. 6s.

**HANDBOOK to the MINERALOGY of CORNWALL and DEVON;** with Instructions for their Discrimination, and copious Tablets of Localities. By J. H. Collins, F.G.S. With 10 Plates. 8vo. 6s.

**PRACTICAL TREATISE on METALLURGY,** adapted from the last German Edition of Professor Kerl's Metallurgy by W. Crookes, F.R.S. &c, and E. Röhrig, Ph.D. M.E. With 625 Woodcuts. 3 vols. 8vo. price £4 19s.

**MITCHELL'S MANUAL of PRACTICAL ASSAYING.** Fourth Edition, for the most part rewritten, with all the recent Discoveries incorporated, by W. Crookes, F.R.S. With 199 Woodcuts. 8vo. 31s. 6d.

**LOUDON'S ENCYCLOPÆDIA of AGRICULTURE:** comprising the Laying-out, Improvement, and Management of Landed Property, and the Cultivation and Economy of Agricultural Produce. With 1,100 Woodcuts. 8vo. 21s.

**Loudon's Encyclopædia of Gardening:** comprising the Theory and Practice of Horticulture, Floriculture, Arboriculture, and Landscape Gardening. With 1,000 Woodcuts. 8vo. 21s.

## *Religious* and *Moral Works.*

**SERMONS**; Including Two Sermons on the Interpretation of Prophecy, and an Essay on the Right Interpretation and Understanding of the Scriptures. By the late Rev. THOMAS ARNOLD, D.D. 3 vols. 8vo. price 24s.

**CHRISTIAN LIFE, its COURSE, its HINDRANCES, and its HELPS**; Sermons preached mostly in the Chapel of Rugby School. By the late Rev. THOMAS ARNOLD, D.D. 8vo. 7s. 6d.

**CHRISTIAN LIFE, its HOPES, its FEARS, and its CLOSE**; Sermons preached mostly in the Chapel of Rugby School. By the late Rev. THOMAS ARNOLD, D.D. 8vo. 7s. 6d.

**SERMONS** chiefly on the **INTERPRETATION** of **SCRIPTURE.** By the late Rev. THOMAS ARNOLD, D.D. 8vo. price 7s. 6d.

**SERMONS** preached in the Chapel of Rugby School; with an Address before Confirmation. By the late Rev. THOMAS ARNOLD, D.D. Fcp. 8vo. price 3s. 6d.

**THREE ESSAYS** on **RELIGION**: Nature; the Utility of Religion; Theism. By JOHN STUART MILL. 8vo. price 10s. 6d.

**INTRODUCTION** to the **SCIENCE** of **RELIGION.** Four Lectures delivered at the Royal Institution; with Two Essays on False Analogies and the Philosophy of Mythology. By F. MAX MÜLLER, M.A. Crown 8vo. 10s. 6d.

**SUPERNATURAL RELIGION**; an Inquiry into the Reality of Divine Revelation. Third Edition, revised. 2 vols. 8vo. 24s.

**ESSAYS** on the **HISTORY** of the **CHRISTIAN RELIGION.** By JOHN Earl RUSSELL. Cabinet Edition, revised. Fcp. 8vo. price 3s. 6d.

**The NEW BIBLE COMMENTARY,** by Bishops and other Clergy of the Anglican Church, critically examined by the Right Rev. J. W. COLENSO, D.D. Bishop of Natal. 8vo. price 25s.

**REASONS** of **FAITH**; or, the ORDER of the Christian Argument Developed and Explained. By the Rev. G. S. DREW, M.A. Second Edition, revised and enlarged. Fcp. 8vo. price 6s.

**SYNONYMS** of the **OLD TESTAMENT,** their **BEARING** on **CHRISTIAN FAITH** and **PRACTICE.** By the Rev. R. B. GIRDLESTONE, M.A. 8vo. 15s.

**An INTRODUCTION** to the **THEOLOGY** of the **CHURCH** of **ENGLAND,** in an Exposition of the Thirty-nine Articles. By the Rev. T. P. BOULTBEE, LL.D. New Edition, Fcp. 8vo. price 6s.

**SERMONS** for the **TIMES** preached in St. Paul's Cathedral and elsewhere. By the Rev. THOMAS GRIFFITH, M.A. Crown 8vo. 6s.

**An EXPOSITION** of the **39 ARTICLES,** Historical and Doctrinal. By E. HAROLD BROWNE, D.D. Lord Bishop of Winchester. New Edit. 8vo. 16s.

**The LIFE and EPISTLES of ST. PAUL.** By the Rev. W. J. CONYBEARE, M.A., and the Very Rev. J. S. HOWSON, D.D. Dean of Chester:—
LIBRARY EDITION, with all the Original Illustrations, Maps, Landscapes on Steel, Woodcuts, &c. 2 vols. 4to. 48s.
INTERMEDIATE EDITION, with a Selection of Maps, Plates, and Woodcuts. 2 vols. square crown 8vo. 21s.
STUDENT'S EDITION, revised and condensed, with 46 Illustrations and Maps. 1 vol. crown 8vo. price 9s.

The **VOYAGE** and **SHIPWRECK** of **ST. PAUL**; with Dissertations on the Life and Writings of St. Luke and the Ships and Navigation of the Ancients. By JAMES SMITH, F.R.S. Third Edition. Crown 8vo. 10s. 6d.

**COMMENTARY** on the **EPISTLE** to the **ROMANS**. By the Rev. W. A. O'CONOR, B.A. Crown 8vo. price 3s. 6d.

The **EPISTLE** to the **HEBREWS**; with Analytical Introduction and Notes. By the Rev. W. A. O'CONOR, B.A. Crown 8vo. price 4s. 6d.

A **CRITICAL** and **GRAMMATICAL COMMENTARY** on **ST. PAUL'S** Epistles. By C. J. ELLICOTT, D.D. Lord Bishop of Gloucester and Bristol. 8vo.

Galatians, Fourth Edition, 8s. 6d.

Ephesians, Fourth Edition, 8s. 6d.

Pastoral Epistles, Fourth Edition, 10s. 6d.

Philippians, Colossians, and Philemon, Third Edition, 10s. 6d.

Thessalonians, Third Edition, 7s. 6d.

**HISTORICAL LECTURES** on the **LIFE** of **OUR LORD**. By C. J. ELLICOTT, D.D. Bishop of Gloucester and Bristol. Fifth Edition. 8vo. 12s.

**EVIDENCE** of the **TRUTH** of the **CHRISTIAN RELIGION** derived from the Literal Fulfilment of Prophecy. By ALEXANDER KEITH, D.D. 37th Edition, with Plates, in square 8vo. 12s. 6d.; 39th Edition, in post 8vo. 6s.

The **HISTORY** and **LITERATURE** of the **ISRAELITES**, according to the Old Testament and the Apocrypha. By C. DE ROTHSCHILD and A. DE ROTHSCHILD. Second Edition, revised. 2 vols. post 8vo. with Two Maps, price 12s. 6d. Abridged Edition, in 1 vol. fcp. 8vo. price 3s. 6d.

An **INTRODUCTION** to the **STUDY** of the **NEW TESTAMENT**, Critical, Exegetical, and Theological. By the Rev. S. DAVIDSON, D.D. LL.D. 2 vols. 8vo. 30s.

**HISTORY** of **ISRAEL**. By H. EWALD, Prof. of the Univ. of Göttingen. Translated by J. E. CARPENTER, M.A., with a Preface by RUSSELL MARTINEAU, M.A. 5 vols. 8vo. 63s.

The **TREASURY** of **BIBLE KNOWLEDGE**; being a Dictionary of the Books, Persons, Places, Events, and other matters of which mention is made in Holy Scripture. By Rev. J. AYRE, M.A. With Maps, 16 Plates, and numerous Woodcuts. Fcp. 8vo. price 6s. cloth, or 10s. neatly bound in calf.

**LECTURES** on the **PENTATEUCH** and the **MOABITE STONE**. By the Right Rev. J. W. COLENSO, D.D. Bishop of Natal. 8vo. 12s.

The **PENTATEUCH** and **BOOK** of **JOSHUA CRITICALLY EXAMINED**. By the Right Rev. J. W. COLENSO, D.D. Bishop of Natal. Crown 8vo. 6s.

**THOUGHTS** for the **AGE**. By ELIZABETH M. SEWELL, Author of 'Amy Herbert,' &c. New Edition, revised. Fcp. 8vo. price 3s. 6d.

**PASSING THOUGHTS** on **RELIGION**. By Miss SEWELL. Fcp. 8vo. 3s. 6d.

**SELF-EXAMINATION** before **CONFIRMATION**. By Miss SEWELL. 32mo. price 1s. 6d.

**READINGS** for a **MONTH** preparatory to **CONFIRMATION**, from Writers of the Early and English Church. By Miss SEWELL. Fcp. 4s.

**READINGS for EVERY DAY in LENT,** compiled from the Writings of Bishop JEREMY TAYLOR. By Miss SEWELL. Fcp. 5s.

**PREPARATION for the HOLY COMMUNION ;** the Devotions chiefly from the Works of JEREMY TAYLOR. By Miss SEWELL. 32mo. 3s.

**THOUGHTS for the HOLY WEEK for Young Persons.** By Miss SEWELL. New Edition. Fcp. 8vo. 2s.

**PRINCIPLES of EDUCATION Drawn from Nature and Revelation,** and applied to Female Education in the Upper Classes. By Miss SEWELL. 2 vols. fcp. 8vo. 12s. 6d.

**LYRA GERMANICA,** Hymns translated from the German by Miss C. WINKWORTH. First and Second Series, price 3s. 6d. each.

**SPIRITUAL SONGS for the SUNDAYS and HOLIDAYS through-** out the Year. By J. S. B. MONSELL, LL.D. Fcp. 8vo. 4s. 6d.

**ENDEAVOURS after the CHRISTIAN LIFE :** Discourses. By the Rev. J. MARTINEAU, LL.D. Fifth Edition, carefully revised. Crown 8vo. 7s. 6d.

**HYMNS of PRAISE and PRAYER,** collected and edited by the Rev. J. MARTINEAU, LL.D. Crown 8vo. 4s. 6d.

**WHATELY'S INTRODUCTORY LESSONS on the CHRISTIAN** Evidences. 18mo. 6d.

**BISHOP JEREMY TAYLOR'S ENTIRE WORKS.** With Life by BISHOP HEBER. Revised and corrected by the Rev. C. P. EDEN. Complete in Ten Volumes, 8vo. cloth, price £5. 5s.

---

## Travels, Voyages, &c.

**EIGHT YEARS in CEYLON.** By Sir SAMUEL W. BAKER, M.A. F.R.G.S. New Edition, with Illustrations engraved on Wood, by G. Pearson. Crown 8vo. 7s. 6d.

**The RIFLE and the HOUND in CEYLON.** By Sir SAMUEL W. BAKER, M.A. F.R.G.S. New Edition, with Illustrations engraved on Wood by G. Pearson. Crown 8vo. 7s. 6d.

**MEETING the SUN ;** a Journey all round the World through Egypt, China, Japan, and California. By WILLIAM SIMPSON, F.R.G.S. With 48 Helio-types and Wood Engravings from Drawings by the Author. Medium 8vo. 34s.

**UNTRODDEN PEAKS and UNFREQUENTED VALLEYS ;** a Mid-summer Ramble among the Dolomites. By AMELIA B. EDWARDS. With a Map and 27 Wood Engravings. Medium 8vo. 21s.

**The DOLOMITE MOUNTAINS ;** Excursions through Tyrol, Carinthia, Carniola, and Friuli, 1861-1863. By J. GILBERT and G. C. CHURCHILL, F.R.G.S. With numerous Illustrations. Square crown 8vo. 21s.

**The VALLEYS of TIROL ;** their Traditions and Customs, and how to Visit them. By Miss R. H. BUSK, Author of 'The Folk-Lore of Rome,' &c. With Maps and Frontispiece. Crown 8vo. 12s. 6d.

**HOURS of EXERCISE in the ALPS.** By JOHN TYNDALL, LL.D.
D.C.L. F.R.S. Third Edition, with 7 Woodcuts by E. Whymper. Crown 8vo.
price 12s. 6d.

**The ALPINE CLUB MAP of SWITZERLAND,** with parts of the
Neighbouring Countries, on the Scale of Four Miles to an Inch. Edited by R.
C. NICHOLS, F.S.A. F.R.G.S. In Four Sheets, price 42s. or mounted in a case,
52s. 6d. Each Sheet may be had separately, price 12s. or mounted in a case, 15s.

**MAP of the CHAIN of MONT BLANC,** from an Actual Survey in
1863–1864. By ADAMS-REILLY, F.R.G.S. M.A.C. Published under the Authority of the Alpine Club. In Chromolithography on extra stout drawing-
paper 28in. × 17in. price 10s. or mounted on canvas in a folding case, 12s. 6d.

**TRAVELS in the CENTRAL CAUCASUS and BASHAN.** Including
Visits to Ararat and Tabreez and Ascents of Kazbek and Elbruz. By D. W.
FRESHFIELD. Square crown 8vo. with Maps, &c. 18s.

**PAU and the PYRENEES.** By Count HENRY RUSSELL, Member of
the Alpine Club, &c. With 2 Maps. Fcp. 8vo. price 5s.

**HOW to SEE NORWAY.** By Captain J. R. CAMPBELL. With Map
and 5 Woodcuts. Fcp. 8vo. price 5s.

**GUIDE to the PYRENEES,** for the use of Mountaineers. By
CHARLES PACKE. With Map and Illustrations. Crown 8vo. 7s. 6d.

**The ALPINE GUIDE.** By JOHN BALL, M.R.I.A. late President of
the Alpine Club. 3 vols. post 8vo. Thoroughly Revised Editions, with Maps
and Illustrations:—I. *Western Alps,* 6s. 6d. II. *Central Alps,* 7s. 6d. III.
*Eastern Alps,* 10s. 6d.

**Introduction on Alpine Travelling in General, and on the Geology**
of the Alps, price 1s. Each of the Three Volumes or Parts of the *Alpine Guide*
may be had with this INTRODUCTION prefixed, price 1s. extra.

**VISITS to REMARKABLE PLACES:** Old Halls, Battle-Fields, and
Scenes Illustrative of Striking Passages in English History and Poetry. By
WILLIAM HOWITT. 2 vols. square crown 8vo. with Woodcuts, 25s.

**The RURAL LIFE of ENGLAND.** By the same Author. With
Woodcuts by Bewick and Williams. Medium 8vo. 12s. 6d.

---

## Works of Fiction.

**WHISPERS from FAIRYLAND.** By the Rt. Hon. E. H. KNATCH-
BULL-HUGESSEN, M.P. Author of 'Stories for my Children,' 'Moonshine,'
'Queer Folk,' &c. With Nine Illustrations from Original Designs engraved on
Wood by G. Pearson. Crown 8vo. price 6s.

**ELENA, an Italian Tale.** By L. N. COMYN, Author of 'Atherstone
Priory.' 2 vols. post 8vo. 14s.

**CENTULLE, a Tale of Pau.** By DENYS SHYNE LAWLOR, Author of
'Pilgrimages in the Pyrenees and Landes. Post 8vo. 10s. 6d.

**LADY WILLOUGHBY'S DIARY, 1635—1663;** Charles the First, the
Protectorate, and the Restoration. Reproduced in the Style of the Period to
which the Diary relates. Crown 8vo. price 7s. 6d.

**TALES of the TEUTONIC LANDS.** By the Rev. G. W. Cox, M.A. and E. H. Jones. Crown 8vo. 10s. 6d.

**The FOLK-LORE of ROME,** collected by Word of Mouth from the People. By Miss R. H. Busk, Author of 'Patrañas,' &c. Crown 8vo. 12s. 6d.

**NOVELS and TALES.** By the Right Hon. B. Disraeli, M.P. Cabinet Edition, complete in Ten Volumes, crown 8vo. price £3.

| | |
|---|---|
| LOTHAIR, 6s. | HENRIETTA TEMPLE, 6s. |
| CONINGSBY, 6s. | CONTARINI FLEMING, &c. 6s. |
| SYBIL, 6s. | ALROY, IXION, &c. 6s. |
| TANCRED, 6s. | The YOUNG DUKE, &c. 6s. |
| VENETIA, 6s. | VIVIAN GREY, 6s. |

**The MODERN NOVELIST'S LIBRARY.** Each Work, in crown 8vo. complete in a Single Volume :—

ATHERSTONE PRIORY, 2s. boards; 2s. 6d. cloth.
MELVILLE'S GLADIATORS, 2s boards; 2s. 6d. cloth.
———— GOOD FOR NOTHING, 2s. boards; 2s. 6d. cloth.
———— HOLMBY HOUSE, 2s. boards; 2s. 6d. cloth.
———— INTERPRETER, 2s. boards; 2s. 6d. cloth.
———— KATE COVENTRY, 2s. boards; 2s. 6d. cloth.
———— QUEEN'S MARIES, 2s. boards; 2s. 6d. cloth.
———— DIGBY GRAND, 2s. boards; 2s. 6d. cloth.
———— GENERAL BOUNCE, 2s. boards; 2s. 6d. cloth.
TROLLOPE'S WARDEN, 1s. 6d. boards; 2s. cloth.
———— BARCHESTER TOWERS, 2s. boards; 2s. 6d. cloth.
BRAMLEY-MOORE'S SIX SISTERS of the VALLEYS, 2s. boards; 2s. 6d. cloth.
The BURGOMASTER'S FAMILY, 2s. boards; 2s. 6d. cloth.

**CABINET EDITION of STORIES and TALES** by Miss Sewell :—

| | |
|---|---|
| AMY HERBERT, 2s. 6d. | IVORS, 2s. 6d. |
| GERTRUDE, 2s. 6d. | KATHARINE ASHTON, 2s. 6d. |
| The EARL'S DAUGHTER, 2s. 6d. | MARGARET PERCIVAL, 3s. 6d. |
| EXPERIENCE of LIFE, 2s. 6d. | LANETON PARSONAGE, 3s. 6d. |
| CLEVE HALL, 2s. 6d. | URSULA, 2s. 6d. |

**CYLLENE**; or, the Fall of Paganism. By Henry Sneyd, M.A. University College, Oxford. 2 vols. post 8vo. price 14s.

**BECKER'S GALLUS;** or, Roman Scenes of the Time of Augustus: with Notes and Excursuses. New Edition. Post 8vo. 7s. 6d.

**BECKER'S CHARICLES;** a Tale illustrative of Private Life among the Ancient Greeks: with Notes and Excursuses. New Edition. Post 8vo. 7s. 6d.

**TALES of ANCIENT GREECE.** By George W. Cox, M.A. late Scholar of Trin. Coll. Oxon. Crown 8vo. price 6s. 6d.

---

## Poetry and *The Drama.*

**FAUST:** a Dramatic Poem. By Goethe. Translated into English Prose, with Notes, by A. Hayward. Ninth Edition. Fcp. 8vo. price 2s.

**MOORE'S IRISH MELODIES,** Maclise's Edition, with 161 Steel Plates from Original Drawings. Super-royal 8vo. 21s. 6d.

**Miniature Edition of Moore's Irish Melodies,** with Maclise's Designs (as above) reduced in Lithography. Imp. 16mo. 10s. 6d.

**BALLADS and LYRICS of OLD FRANCE;** with other Poems. By
A. LANG, Fellow of Merton College, Oxford. Square fcp. 8vo. price 5s.

**MOORE'S LALLA ROOKH.** Tenniel's Edition, with 68 Wood
Engravings from Original Drawings and other Illustrations. Fcp. 4to. 21s.

**SOUTHEY'S POETICAL WORKS,** with the Author's last Corrections
and copyright Additions. Medium 8vo. with Portrait and Vignette, 14s.

**LAYS of ANCIENT ROME; with IVRY and the ARMADA.** By the
Right Hon. Lord MACAULAY. 16mo. 3s. 6d.

**LORD MACAULAY'S LAYS of ANCIENT ROME.** With 90 Illustrations on Wood, from the Antique, from Drawings by G. SCHARF. Fcp. 4to. 21s.

**Miniature Edition of Lord Macaulay's Lays of Ancient Rome,**
with the Illustrations (as above) reduced in Lithography. Imp. 16mo. 10s. 6d.

**The ÆNEID of VIRGIL** Translated into English Verse. By JOHN
CONINGTON, M.A. New Edition. Crown 8vo. 9s.

**HORATII OPERA.** Library Edition, with Marginal References and
English Notes. Edited by the Rev. J. E. YONGE. 8vo. 21s.

**The LYCIDAS and EPITAPHIUM DAMONIS of MILTON.** Edited,
with Notes and Introduction (including a Reprint of the rare Latin Version
of the Lycidas, by W. Hogg, 1694), by C. S. JERRAM, M.A. Crown 8vo. 3s. 6d.

**BOWDLER'S FAMILY SHAKSPEARE,** cheaper Genuine Editions.
Medium 8vo. large type, with 36 Woodcuts, price 14s. Cabinet Edition, with
the same ILLUSTRATIONS, 6 vols. fcp. 8vo. price 21s.

**POEMS.** By JEAN INGELOW. 2 vols. fcp. 8vo. price 10s.
FIRST SERIES, containing ' DIVIDED,' ' The STAR'S MONUMENT,' &c. Sixteenth
Thousand. Fcp. 8vo. price 5s.
SECOND SERIES, ' A STORY of DOOM,' ' GLADYS and her ISLAND,' &c. Fifth
Thousand. Fcp. 8vo. price 5s.

**POEMS by Jean Ingelow.** FIRST SERIES, with nearly 100 Illustrations,
engraved on Wood by Dalziel Brothers. Fcp. 4to. 21s.

## Rural Sports, &c.

**DOWN the ROAD;** Or, Reminiscences of a Gentleman Coachman.
By C. T. S. BIRCH REYNARDSON. With Twelve Chromolithographic Illustrations from Original Paintings by H. Alken. Medium 8vo. [Nearly ready.

**The DEAD SHOT;** or, Sportsman's Complete Guide: a Treatise on
the Use of the Gun, Dog-breaking, Pigeon-shooting, &c. By MARKSMAN.
Revised Edition. Fcp. 8vo. with Plates, 5s.

**ENCYCLOPÆDIA of RURAL SPORTS;** a complete Account, Historical, Practical, and Descriptive, of Hunting, Shooting, Fishing, Racing,
and all other Rural and Athletic Sports and Pastimes. By D. P. BLAINE.
With above 600 Woodcuts (20 from Designs by JOHN LEECH). 8vo. 21s.

The **FLY-FISHER'S ENTOMOLOGY.** By ALFRED RONALDS. With coloured Representations of the Natural and Artificial Insect. Sixth Edition, with 20 coloured Plates. 8vo. 14s.

A **BOOK** on **ANGLING**; a complete Treatise on the Art of Angling in every branch. By FRANCIS FRANCIS. New Edition, with Portrait and 15 other Plates, plain and coloured. Post 8vo. 15s.

**WILCOCKS'S SEA-FISHERMAN**; comprising the Chief Methods of Hook and Line Fishing, a Glance at Nets, and Remarks on Boats and Boating. New Edition, with 80 Woodcuts. Post 8vo. 12s. 6d.

**HORSES** and **STABLES.** By Colonel F. FITZWYGRAM, XV. the King's Hussars. With Twenty-four Plates of Illustrations, containing very numerous Figures engraved on Wood. 8vo. 10s. 6d.

The **HORSE'S FOOT,** and **HOW to KEEP It SOUND.** By W. MILES, Esq. Ninth Edition, with Illustrations. Imperial 8vo. 12s. 6d.

A **PLAIN TREATISE** on **HORSE-SHOEING.** By W. MILES, Esq. Sixth Edition. Post 8vo. with Illustrations, 2s. 6d.

**STABLES** and **STABLE-FITTINGS.** By W. MILES, Esq. Imp. 8vo. with 13 Plates, 15s.

**REMARKS** on **HORSES' TEETH,** addressed to Purchasers. By W. MILES, Esq. Post 8vo. 1s. 6d.

A **TREATISE** on **HORSE-SHOEING** and **LAMENESS.** By JOSEPH GAMGEE, Veterinary Surgeon. 8vo. with 55 Woodcuts, price 10s. 6d.

The **HORSE**: with a Treatise on Draught. By WILLIAM YOUATT. New Edition, revised and enlarged. 8vo. with numerous Woodcuts, 12s. 6d.

The **DOG.** By WILLIAM YOUATT. 8vo. with numerous Woodcuts, 6s.

The **DOG** in **HEALTH** and **DISEASE.** By STONEHENGE. With 70 Wood Engravings. Square crown 8vo. 7s. 6d.

The **GREYHOUND.** By STONEHENGE. Revised Edition, with 24 Portraits of Greyhounds. Square crown 8vo. 10s. 6d.

The **OX**; his Diseases and their Treatment: with an Essay on Parturition in the Cow. By J. R. DOBSON. Crown 8vo. with Illustrations, 7s. 6d.

---

## Works of Utility and General Information.

The **THEORY** and **PRACTICE** of **BANKING.** By H. D. MACLEOD, M.A. Barrister-at-Law. Second Edition, entirely remodelled. 2 vols. 8vo. 30s.

**M'CULLOCH'S DICTIONARY,** Practical, Theoretical, and Historical, of Commerce and Commercial Navigation. New and revised Edition. 8vo. 63s.

The **CABINET LAWYER**; a Popular Digest of the Laws of England, Civil, Criminal, and Constitutional: intended for Practical Use and General Information. Twenty-fourth Edition. Fcp. 8vo. price 9s.

**BLACKSTONE ECONOMISED**, a Compendium of the Laws of England to the Present time, in Four Books, each embracing the Legal Principles and Practical Information contained in their respective volumes of Blackstone, supplemented by Subsequent Statutory Enactments, Important Legal Decisions, &c. By D. M. AIRD, Barrister-at-Law. Revised Edition. Post 8vo. 7s. 6d.

**PEWTNER'S COMPREHENSIVE SPECIFIER;** a Guide to the Practical Specification of every kind of Building-Artificers' Work, with Forms of Conditions and Agreements. Edited by W. YOUNG. Crown 8vo. 6s.

**COLLIERIES and COLLIERS;** a Handbook of the Law and Leading Cases relating thereto. By J. C. FOWLER. Third Edition. Fcp. 8vo. 7s. 6d.

**HINTS to MOTHERS** on the **MANAGEMENT** of their **HEALTH** during the Period of Pregnancy and in the Lying-in Room. By the late THOMAS BULL, M.D. Fcp. 8vo. 5s.

The **MATERNAL MANAGEMENT of CHILDREN** in **HEALTH** and Disease. By the late THOMAS BULL, M.D. Fcp. 8vo. 5s.

The **THEORY** of the **MODERN SCIENTIFIC GAME** of **WHIST.** By WILLIAM POLE, F.R.S. Fifth Edition, enlarged. Fcp. 8vo. 2s. 6d.

**CHESS OPENINGS.** By F. W. LONGMAN, Balliol College, Oxford. Second Edition revised. Fcp. 8vo. 2s. 6d.

**THREE HUNDRED ORIGINAL CHESS PROBLEMS and STUDIES.** By JAMES PIERCE, M.A. and W. T. PIERCE. With numerous Diagrams. Square fcp. 8vo. 7s. 6d. SUPPLEMENT, price 2s. 6d.

**A PRACTICAL TREATISE** on **BREWING;** with Formulæ for Public Brewers, and Instructions for Private Families. By W. BLACK. 8vo. 10s. 6d.

**MODERN COOKERY for PRIVATE FAMILIES,** reduced to a System of Easy Practice in a Series of carefully-tested Receipts. By ELIZA ACTON. Newly revised and enlarged; with 8 Plates and 150 Woodcuts. Fcp. 8vo. 6s.

**MAUNDER'S TREASURY of KNOWLEDGE** and **LIBRARY** of Reference; comprising an English Dictionary and Grammar, Universal Gazetteer, Classical Dictionary, Chronology, Law Dictionary, a synopsis of the Peerage useful Tables, &c. Revised Edition. Fcp. 8vo. 6s. cloth, or 10s. calf.

---

## Knowledge for the Young.

The **STEPPING-STONE to KNOWLEDGE;** or upwards of 700 Questions and Answers on Miscellaneous Subjects, adapted to the capacity of Infant minds. 18mo. 1s.

**SECOND SERIES of the STEPPING-STONE to KNOWLEDGE:** Containing upwards of 800 Questions and Answers on Miscellaneous Subjects not contained in the FIRST SERIES. 18mo. 1s.

The **STEPPING-STONE to GEOGRAPHY:** Containing several Hundred Questions and Answers on Geographical Subjects. 18mo. 1s

The **STEPPING-STONE to ENGLISH HISTORY**; Questions and Answers on the History of England. 18mo. 1s.

The **STEPPING-STONE to BIBLE KNOWLEDGE**; Questions and Answers on the Old and New Testaments. 18mo. 1s.

The **STEPPING-STONE to BIOGRAPHY**; Questions and Answers on the Lives of Eminent Men and Women. 18mo. 1s.

The **STEPPING-STONE to IRISH HISTORY**: Containing several Hundred Questions and Answers on the History of Ireland. 18mo. 1s.

The **STEPPING-STONE to FRENCH HISTORY**: Containing several Hundred Questions and Answers on the History of France. 18mo. 1s.

The **STEPPING-STONE to ROMAN HISTORY**: Containing several Hundred Questions and Answers on the History of Rome. 18mo. 1s.

The **STEPPING-STONE to GRECIAN HISTORY**: Containing several Hundred Questions and Answers on the History of Greece. 18mo. 1s.

The **STEPPING-STONE to ENGLISH GRAMMAR**: Containing several Hundred Questions and Answers on English Grammar. 18mo. 1s.

The **STEPPING-STONE to FRENCH PRONUNCIATION and CON-VERSATION**: Containing several Hundred Questions and Answers. 18mo. 1s.

The **STEPPING-STONE to ASTRONOMY**: Containing several Hundred familiar Questions and Answers on the Earth and the Solar and Stellar Systems. 18mo. 1s.

The **STEPPING-STONE to MUSIC**: Containing several Hundred Questions on the Science; also a short History of Music. 18mo. 1s.

The **STEPPING-STONE to NATURAL HISTORY**: VERTEBRATE OR BACK-BONED ANIMALS. PART I. *Mammalia*; PART II. *Birds, Reptiles, Fishes.* 18mo. 1s. each Part.

THE **STEPPING-STONE to ARCHITECTURE**; Questions and Answers explaining the Principles and Progress of Architecture from the Earliest Times. With 100 Woodcuts. 18mo. 1s.

# INDEX.